1

CHERRY CAKE
and a
CADAVER

by Susan Boles

An Argent Ocean Publishing book

Copyright 2017

Praise for the
Lily Gayle Lambert Mystery Series

"...a charming southern cozy chocked full of engaging characters, laugh out loud humor, and inviting small town charm." Kathi Daley, Author of the Zoe Donovan Cozy Mysteries

"...fast-paced and funny. A true Southern mystery with a flavor as authentic as sweet tea." Jenna Bennett, Author of the Savannah Martin mysteries.

"...Ms. Boles is a master baker of cozy mysteries. The multiple story elements are mixed together just right and make Cherry Cake and a Cadaver a worthy addition to the series and a tasty read in its own right." Back Porchervations

"The characters are always well done and the setting described where the reader thinks they are in the story. You will find yourself turning the pages quickly to see what kind of trouble Lily gets herself into. The secondary characters are just as good and keep the laughter flowing. You will be kept guessing until the end." Babs Book Bistro

"The characters are well rounded and well developed. Lily Gayle is smart, sassy and a well bred Southern woman. With the reluctant help of her friend, Dixie, she is determined to solve the case. Lily Gayle and Dixie's friendship is so funny and so heartwarming. I think that their relationship is one of my favorites in all of cozyville". Mary Brown, reader

CHAPTER ONE

"The Midnight Dragonfly." Miss Edna snorted. "I never heard the like."

I set my rocking chair in motion, enjoying the rhythmic sound of the rockers against the old wooden porch. I'd come over to visit with Miss Edna and we'd ended up out here on her big porch, sharing a pitcher of sweet tea and enjoying the spring sunshine and slight breeze.

I thought nostalgically of the sound of slapping screen doors that had marked spring and summer when I was coming up.

That *twang-thwack* sound could transport me right back to my childhood, but I wouldn't be hearing one of those anytime soon. Even here in Mercy, people had changed over to security doors, and what was lost in culture didn't figure into our lives anymore.

Miss Edna loved sitting on this big ole front porch with it's view of the town square. She needed to keep an eye on the activities of friends and neighbors. Her usual binoculars weren't hanging from her neck today, though. No doubt she thought she was fooling me by not wearing them. Even without them, her eyes stayed busy marking the progress and destination of everyone on the square as we talked.

Since I knew her to be almost blind as a bat, I spent a minute wondering how she knew who everyone was. But she never mixed up anybody, so she must have some superpower I hadn't discovered as of yet. Our current topic of conversation centered around the new bed-and-breakfast scheduled to open next weekend.

"I suppose the new owner wanted a name that sounded romantic and authentically Southern," I answered.

Miss Edna wasn't one to roll her eyes, but I sensed a mental eye roll from her direction. "Well, if that's the case, they should be calling it the Midnight Snake Doctor. That's what real, *authentic* Southerners calls dragonflies. At least the ones from *my* generation. I reckon maybe you don't call them that."

I laughed. "Somehow Midnight Snake Doctor just doesn't have the same sense of the ritzy as Midnight Dragonfly."

"Too highfalutin for this town," Miss Edna replied, tapping her fingers on the table between us. Then, motioning outward with her hand, she added. "Just like the restaurant over there on the square being called Grits and Gravy. Well, Joe's Café was good enough for their grandparents, and their parents too. Why did they need to name it something so ridiculous anyway?"

I picked up my glass of tea, feeling a slight sheen of sweat on it even this early in the year from the temperature outside. I hoped it wasn't an omen for a hellishly hot summer.

I took a sip, letting the sweetness trickle down my throat. Nothing better on a spring morning than a glass of perfectly made sweet tea. And Miss Edna was a master. She sure seemed to be in a mood today though.

"The town has been getting some traffic off the interstate the last few years." I said. "The kids just want to keep the place in business. People on their way between New York and Florida want to eat at places with authentic-sounding Southern names."

Miss Edna snorted again. "Well, they aren't getting them. These fancy-dancy names are just some made-up crap. *Real* old time Southern places don't have names like that. And I don't like strangers stopping in town anyway. Brings down the tone of the place to have people with no history browsing through here like it's Disneyland or something."

As I smothered a laugh into a fake cough, her eyes darted sharply to my left. I subtly tried cutting my own eyes in that direction with no results. Well, shoot. Whatever had her attention was too far past my line of vision.

I casually shifted in my chair, pretending to recross my legs. Ah. Harley Ann, Miss Edna's great-niece, and Bobby Moore, the local bad boy, strolling across the city park, disappearing behind the gazebo. I casually shifted my position again, recrossed my legs and looked at Miss Edna, who had a very sour expression on her face. Oops. Was that for me or Harley Ann? I fought the urge to squirm.

"Damn fool girl," I heard her mutter quietly.

"So, who do you think the new owners are?" I said to distract her.

She stopped staring holes in the direction of the gazebo and turned her gaze back to me.

"Probably some damn Yankees since they don't have the first idea about naming things." She cast a dark glance back in the direction of the gazebo.

"How do you reckon these Yankees found out the old Mitchell Manor was for sale?"

"How does anybody find out about anything?"

"Well, around here it's mostly at the beauty shop." I thought back over the past months and nothing came to mind out of the ordinary. "I haven't seen any mysterious Yankees lurking around outside it, or in there getting their hair done and soaking up all the local gossip either." I paused for a minute, remembering how hot that topic had been for a long time. Then I shook my head. Nope. Couldn't have been from the It'll Grow Back, my best friend Dixie's hair salon down on the square.

I looked in that direction, thinking I needed to make an appointment to get my roots touched up. Going around with a skunk stripe just isn't done. I fingered the part in my hair, wondering if a glimmer of silver might be showing along the scalp. I should've taken a closer look in the mirror this morning when I was drying my hair. It'd been a few weeks since my last visit to the beauty shop.

"What are you doing?" Miss Edna asked. "You're drivin' me crazy with that fidgeting. Put your hands in your lap and stop it." With an evil little smirk, she added, "Your roots are showing. Better get on over to Dixie's your own self."

I refused to be drawn by her and put my hands under my thighs to make sure I didn't start messing with my hair again. "But, really, where do you think they found out about the place being up for sale?"

"Have some sense, Lily Gayle. It was in the paper for a month about the wolf man and the murders."

"I don't imagine anybody outside Mercy reads *The Argus*,"" I shot back in exasperation.

"Who's talkin' about that old rag? I'm talking about

the Memphis paper. Don't you remember they swarmed down here like a bunch of locusts once it got out about all that mess?"

I chewed that over for a minute, thinking she was probably right. There'd been a whole circus down here for a week after the murder. A real live wolf man getting murdered in a tiny Mississippi town had been big news. Add to it that the dead wolf man had been a member of the founding family and it just got bigger from there.

We'd all felt like we were under siege during those weeks. But the uproar and fascination finally died down, leaving us to get on with our lives in the usual way.

But all that still didn't explain how someone from away knew Mitchell Manor had gone on the market. Sure, Missy Halbert, the local real estate agent, had listed it online, but I was hard-pressed to figure out why someone would be looking for a big place like that in rural Mississippi.

In the last few years our town had been experiencing something of a small revival, with some increase in tourist traffic, because some of the younger generation had opted to stay home and open small businesses on the town square. I suppose you could stretch it to include out-of-towners looking for a business opportunity. It still seemed odd to me though.

"They must be rich as Croesus," I told Miss Edna, referring to the unknown new owners of the Midnight

Dragonfly. "Billy Larsen's the contractor for some of the work, and his wife told the girls at Dixie's shop that all the improvements they're making would knock your socks off. I can't wait to see it myself."

"Humph." Miss Edna picked up an old school cardboard fan on a stick with a picture of Jesus on it and fanned her face. "You couldn't pay me to go off up there among all the crowd I expect will be there showing off to each other. It'll be everybody and their brother, and I don't cotton to that kind of crowd."

I had a disconcerting vision of Scarlett O'Hara fanning herself and saying "Fiddle dee dee!" I shook my head to get rid of it. Eeew!

"Everybody likes to have a little fun now and then." I stated. "And this bed-and-breakfast is the biggest thing to hit Mercy in a century. Even if it is being run by a bunch of Yankees. Which we don't even know for sure."

"Luxen Natolovich is going to be the pastry chef there," Miss Edna said with a sly look.

"What!? How do you know that?"

"You mean you girls haven't rooted that information out over to the beauty shop? For shame! Y'all are a bunch of amateurs after all."

I could see from the expression on her face she wasn't about to tell me anything else about it. How could Miss Edna have gotten hold of that nugget of information without the rest of us finding out? Oh, it was killin' me! Miss Edna just rocked, cool as a cucumber and gleeful as a child. She'd one-upped me on this one for sure.

I stood up, stretching my back. "Well, I'm gonna go on home now. I'll call Dixie later and set up an appointment for my hair. I can't be walking around with my roots showing."

"You aren't fooling me one little bit, Lily Gayle Lambert. You're rushin' off to start callin' folks to discuss this latest piece of information. You just be sure you let them know it was me that told you." She shook a crooked index finger at me. "Don't you be tryin' to take credit for it."

Head held high, I strolled down her front steps, not dignifying her remark with an answer. But I could still hear her cackling behind me.

CHAPTER TWO

"Aunt Edna says he doesn't have a pot to piss in or a window to throw it out of and I need to set my sights higher than Bobby Moore," Harley Ann said from the comfort of the love seat in my living room.

She heaved a deep sigh like she'd resigned herself to her great-aunt's wishes. But I could see signs of rebellion in the set of her lips and around her eyes. I figured Miss Edna hadn't seen the signs yet. But then, my eyesight's a good deal better than Miss Edna's. At eighty, she was batting a thousand to find her glasses and punch the numbers on her oversize phone. I still couldn't figure out how she managed to raise those darn prizewinning dahlias every year and be blind as a bat. Maybe witchcraft. It wouldn't surprise me a bit.

I made a mental note to keep an eye on Harley Ann's activities. I didn't have a thing in the world against Bobby Moore, but he was a bad boy to the core. A heartbreaker looking for the next fun thing. Having had a soft spot for bad boys myself when I was as young as Harley Ann, I knew what kind of trouble the girl could get in to. And a broken heart might be the least of it.

Talk on the grapevine said Harley Ann had come to live with Miss Edna—who was her great-aunt on her momma's side—under mysterious circumstances. Well, they were mysterious to me and everybody else in town. The story went that Harley Ann had come to take care of her great-aunt who needed someone to stay with her.

Which was just hogwash. Miss Edna was about as frail as a wild boar. And didn't like anyone nosyin' in her personal business. Others might be buying that cockamamie story, but not me. I'd find out the truth sooner or later. There's more than one way to skin a cat after all. But I put it aside for today. No point in upsetting Harley Ann any more than she already was.

"Don't ignore everything your Aunt Edna tells you. She's a smart old biddy." At the younger woman's astonished stare, I added, "What? You know I love her to death and don't mean any disrespect by that. And while I don't think you should stop spending time with Bobby because he doesn't have money, I do agree with Miss Edna that he might not be the right young man for you."

Hurt filled Harley Ann's big blue eyes. "Well, I surely thought you'd be on my side in this, Lily Gayle."

"You did?"

"Well, yes." She sat up, spine straight, on the love seat. "You're always standing up to my aunt and telling her to mind her own business instead of yours. I thought sure you'd understand that I don't want her minding my business either."

Okay. That was true. But I that didn't make a bit of difference in my opinion. I might tell Miss Edna to stay out of my business, but I'm a grown woman with a lot of life experience. I feel like I've earned the right. But, thinking it over and remembering myself at her age, I knew she felt the same way. Maybe she didn't have a lot of life experience, but she *was* a grown woman.

"I do understand all that, hon. I just happen to agree with her on this particular subject." Time to change the subject since this happened to be a battle I'd never win.

I glanced at the brown paper bag in her hand. She'd brought it in with her, and then we'd gotten onto the topic of Bobby Moore before I could ask her what she had. At this point the top of the bag was twisted tighter than Dick's hatband. Poor girl. It was the pits to be young an in love with all the adults in your life ranged against you.

Motioning toward the bag, I asked. "What have you got there?"

Defeated, Harley Ann looked at her hand like she'd forgotten what she had. "Oh. I clean forgot. This is a little jar of some of my flavored butter." She pulled a small Mason jar out of the bag, unscrewed the ring and eased the top off. "Here. Smell."

She walked over to me and I leaned over to sniff the creamy beige substance dotted with tiny reddish-brown spots. "Why, it smells like cinnamon and honey."

Harley Ann smiled. "Do you have some biscuits handy? It's best on those. But you can eat it out of the jar if you don't have any biscuits. Or even on toast if you want."

We moved to my kitchen at the back of the house, bright with sunlight even though the sun had moved over the house. I loved having tea here in the mornings, watching the sun come up and listening to the bird chorus as I planned my day.

Harley Ann sat at the big wooden table by the windows looking out into the woods behind my house as I pulled an antique silver teaspoon out of a drawer in the solid oak sideboard my great great grandparents had brought from North Carolina when they migrated here.

"I don't have any biscuits left over from breakfast," I said as I moved toward her. "But I'm dying to taste it."

I sat down across from her and pulled the little jar closer. Dipping the spoon into the butter, I filled it about half full. Harley Ann watched every move with an anxious expression.

I touched the spoon to my lips, then put the whole

thing in my mouth and licked. The flavor exploded on my tongue and ran right on down to my taste buds, where it did a happy dance among them.

"Wow! This is really good, Harley Ann. Did you make it?"

Ducking her head and not quite hiding the blush staining her cheeks, she said, "Yes, I did. This one is cinnamon, vanilla and honey. I have a whole bunch of different flavors I've created. And some jams, too."

"Where did you learn to make them?" I licked a stray taste off my lips and savored it.

Harley Ann avoided looking me in the eye, fidgeted her hands across the table, crumpling the linen placement in front of her, then straightening it. Her tongue peeked out and wet her lips. Just as I was about to give up, she answered.

"Um. I had some time on my hands a few years ago and I got interested in it." she winced a bit.

Well, how mysterious. But if she didn't want to tell me, I could live with that. As long as she kept me supplied with the stuff.

"Well, this is about the best butter I've ever tasted." I scooped up another spoonful and ate it with relish. "Have you thought about selling it?"

Harley Ann's looked relieved that I wasn't going to hold her feet to the fire on how she'd come to start making her butters. Then, head tilted so low she appeared to be speaking directly to her chest so that I had to strain to hear her, she answered. "Yes, ma'am. I went to see Luxen at the bakery and he showed me the door pretty quick."

Still savoring the taste of the butter on my tongue, I said. "That doesn't sound like Luxen. Maybe he was just having a bad day or something. I'll go have a word with him and see what's going on."

The girl looked up. Beamed. "Would you? I'd be so grateful if you'd do that. Aunt Edna offered to go over and give him a piece of her mind, but I managed to talk her out of it. She meant well, but I didn't want her to make it worse than it already was. I was plannin' on going back myself, but if you go, then maybe it'll all work out for me."

The thought of Miss Edna giving Luxen a piece of her mind gave me a mental smile. The old lady would sure chew him a new one. And he'd never know what hit him. But, as Harley Ann had already pointed out, it wouldn't get her any closer to marketing her wonderful butters.

And I did feel kinda bad that I couldn't take her side on the Bobby Moore thing.

CHAPTER THREE

On the way to Luxen's bakery, I mentally reviewed what Harley Ann had told me. I'd never known Luxen to be rude to anyone and couldn't imagine why he'd start with Harley Ann. Had he heard some of the wild gossip floating around town about her background and believed she'd be a bad investment of his time? Hard to believe, though.

As long as he'd lived in Mercy, Luxen hadn't had close friends. And he didn't strike me as the kind who listened to idle gossip. Nice as the day was long when you went into his business. But I'd never seen him in the Grits and Gravy. Or anywhere else social. Just occasionally at the grocery store or post office.

Poor old guy. Maybe he was just busy with something to do with the opening of the Midnight Dragonfly when she went by and shooed her out so he could take care of it. The flavored butters would be a great addition for him, probably bring in more customers to buy biscuits, so it didn't make sense to me that he wouldn't even give her the time of day about them.

The stuff surely tasted wonderful. I draw a breath, remembering the combination of honey, cinnamon and vanilla doing a slow dance on my tongue from the little bitty sample I'd had. Mm, mm, mm.

Good thing I'd stashed the container in the fridge. I'd definitely be havin' some of it when I got back home. Maybe on a couple of waffles this time. Yes. And some fried chicken to go with it.

The string of little brass bells hanging above the door jingled my arrival as I pushed open the door to the bakery. All kinds of good scents rushed to greet me. Maybe I'd buy some nice pastries to take home with me even, though the waistband on my jeans had been pleading for mercy lately. I'd gotten completely out of my long-walks habit since the mess with the wolf man.

I tried to suck in my stomach with not much result and made a mental note to get back to walking every day. And, hey, Rome wasn't built in a day. And sometimes a girl just needed something sweet. I eyed the full shelves under the big glass showcase.

Luxen came out of the back of the shop wiping something off his hands with a snowy white flour sack towel. My favorite kind. They were the best kind to wipe with. They could soak up a whole world of stuff to be as thin as they were. I'd tossed all my thick, pretty, but not really absorbent kitchen towels and started buying only the flour sack ones years ago.

"What can I do for you, Lily Gayle?' He was gazing over my shoulder, presumably out the big plate-glass window overlooking the street. I shifted over to put myself in his line of vision.

His eyes met mine just for a second and moved away again. "I've got some bear claws. Fresh made this morning," he said to the wall behind me.

What in the world could be wrong with him? I could understand how a young girl like Harley Ann might be put off by his manner, but I was made of sterner stuff.

"I'd love to get some of those bear claws, and some of the croissants in the case. But first—"

He moved quickly to open the case from his side and began shuffling croissants into a white paper bag. I frowned. Where was the friendly, talkative man I knew?

"Luxen. Please stop for a minute." I called to him. "I want to talk to you about Miss Edna's niece, Harley Ann."

He paused for just a second, then kept shoving croissants into the bag. There must be over a dozen in there by now.

"I don't have time to train a silly young girl with her butters. I'll be too busy with my new job at the Inn and running this bakery."

"Luxen!" I said in a loud voice. "Stop!"

He stopped. And, never raising his eyes to mine, twisted the top of the sack tight and put it on top of the glass case.

"I tasted one of her butter creations and it was absolutely delicious," I said to the top of his head. "They could really bring in more business. And she'd be a big help to you. She can run the bakery for you when you have to be up at the Inn."

Finally, he raised his eyes to mine and I saw such a level of sadness there that I wanted to rush around that big old glass counter and give him a hug.

He broke the mood pretty quick, though. "I told you. I don't have time to train a silly young girl. There's nothing for her here. Tell her to go to the café or one of those quaint little shops opening on the square." He shook his head. "So many changes in recent years. So many new faces in town. I thought the world would never come knocking on the door of this little town."

"Well, what's wrong with that?" I asked in exasperation. "It means new life and opportunity for the town. Kids can stay and raise their families here instead of going off somewhere else."

His silver-blue eyes met mine again. "You're right. It is good for the town. I'm an old man and my life is lived already. My choices made long ago." He pushed the white bag toward me. "Take these. No charge. Go." And, with that, headed into the back of the shop. I heard a door slam somewhere back there. Probably to his living quarters upstairs.

I took the bag and stepped out to the street. Well, that was the strangest encounter I'd ever had with Luxen. He'd always been so friendly and talkative in the shop. He remembered every fact, name and family situation. Always made polite conversation with everyone. So why was he suddenly sullen and rude? Was he really so busy that he couldn't take on some help in the shop and at the same time help someone get a small business off the ground? Was something else going on?

He'd seemed so alone and sad. I knew he'd never talk to me about it if there was something wrong. He'd made it clear with his chilly demeanor in the bakery.

It was a puzzle, and I felt equally bad about not understanding why he'd undergone such a personality change and not convincing him to give Harley Ann a chance. He'd made some interesting suggestions about other places she might be able to get a start. I didn't think any of those stores would be good options, though. She'd have to have fancy containers and labeling to do that, and I didn't think she had the money to make an investment like that.

Of course, I could loan her the money. And Miss Edna

might have some cash stashed back somewhere—likely in the mattress, knowing her. But those options didn't seem right somehow. Plus, I had a feeling there might be some kind of legal ramifications with selling food.

Because there really was no way for me to figure it out right then, I pulled a croissant from the bag and bit into it. Sinfully delicious. And I couldn't wait to get home to try it out with some of Harley Ann's cinnamon honey butter.

CHAPTER FOUR

Taking a break from my latest reenactor gown—the Civil War this time—I decided to go on up to Mitchell Manor—I couldn't quite call it Midnight Dragonfly just yet—and peek in the windows to get a feel for the changes that had been made. After all, I *did* need to get back to my walking routine. And I needed a destination for it.

And, since it would be opening in two days, all the workers would be gone and there wouldn't be anyone to see me having my little look-around. I headed on over to Dixie's shop to get her to go with me. It would be just like the old days, us sneaking out together.

"I don't know why I let you talk me into this stuff," Dixie complained as we eased our way up the hill to the Midnight Dragonfly a little while later.

She'd been taking a rare afternoon off from the shop when I stopped by to see her, so she hadn't had the excuse of client appointments to put me off my mission. It must be in the stars for us to go, right? Otherwise she'd have had a book full of appointments and not been able to go. Of course, I'd have gone by myself, but this was way better to my mind.

The early afternoon quiet felt kinda eerie to me, though. I didn't hear a peep out of any birds or animals you'd expect to find out here in the woods outside of town. Maybe we'd scared them silent. Even though we were trying to be quiet. No wind moved through the trees either. Just Dixie and me, trying to step quietly in the mess of old leaves on the ground and, to my mind, sounding like a herd of buffalo announcing our arrival to anyone who might be listening.

You'd think I felt like we were up to something illegal with all those negative thoughts buzzing through my head. But it wasn't like that at all. Really. There's no harm in window peeping and empty house that's pretty much a new construction with no one living there.

As we came to the edge of the woods, I caught glimpses of the old sandstone and granite mansion sitting at the top of the hill. Not much cover between here and there, but I didn't see anyone around, so we should be OK out in the open. Then I wondered why I even had those thoughts. Hadn't I just given myself a bunch of reasons why this was perfectly okay?

"You know you, you're just as curious as I am to see

the changes," I replied to her statement about dragging her into this little adventure.

She sniffed. "The difference is, *I* can wait till the party."

I heard her panting just a bit as we walked on up the hill. Guess ol' Dixie needed to get out of the shop more often and get some exercise. The teenage track star who'd run like the wind had disappeared somewhere along the way. Probably hanging out in the mists of time with the swimming champion I'd once been.

"Well, if you feel that way, why did you come with me?"

She gave me a sardonic smile. "To keep you out of trouble, like I always do."

I rolled my eyes. "Oh, please. There's no trouble to get into today. Besides, don't you want to take it all in without a crowd of people around? You won't be able to stir 'em with a stick at the grand opening. This way we can relax and see it all without having to stop and chat every dozen steps."

"Whew!' Dixie whooshed out a big breath "I need to get back in shape. Walking up this hill is bout near knocking the breath out of me." She twisted from side to side at the waist as we paused to take in the exterior changes.

Though there didn't seem to be any changes to the house itself, the drive had been paved and widened and a big section of the front lawn had been turned into an area for guests to unload their luggage before taking their cars around back to where a covered parking area had been built.

Kind of an eyesore, in my opinion. But I suppose there had to be somewhere to park cars. Maybe they'd put in some nice big shrubbery later to soften the look of it. I briefly wondered if they'd have valet parking. Rumor around town had it the place was going to be very uptown. So maybe they would.

"Lord have mercy," Dixie breathed pulling me from my thoughts. "I bet the Mitchells are rollin' in their graves at all this."

"Considering what we found out about them a few months back, I'd say this isn't bugging them in the least."

I strolled on up toward the house so I could start peeking in windows. I figured the place was locked up tight, but most of the first-floor windows were big and close enough to the ground that we'd be able to see in without too much trouble. Dixie shuffled her feet alongside me, head rotating side to side.

"What the heck are you looking for?" I asked.

""Just keeping an eye out."

"For what?"

Dixie shrugged her shoulders. "Anything or anybody that might be lurking around."

"I swear, Dixie Newsom, you have the most paranoid imagination of anybody I know."

"Considering the kind of stuff that tends to happen when we're sneaking around places we don't belong, it's a wonder I'm not in a psych ward."

I bumped my shoulder against hers. "Stop that exaggerating. Nothing serious has happened." I scanned the area myself. Trying to see behind the trees and bushes lining the drive and in the woods across from us. "Besides. This is public property. We have every right to be here."

Dixie rolled her eyes. "Nothing has happened *yet*, you mean. And it isn't officially open, so we're sneaking around on *private* property."

"When did you become a lawyer?" I asked and marched right on up to the front porch and over to one of the windows. Turning back, I saw Dixie still standing on the lawn. "Oh, come on," I hollered back at her. "You're already here, so you might as well come see, too."

Dixie eased up onto the porch like she thought some kind alarm was going to go off or a cage drop from the porch ceiling, trapping us inside. Together, we cupped our hands around our eyes and peeked into the first window.

Since the blinds were mostly drawn, we had to do a little bobbing dance to get a glimpse inside. I'd only been in there that one time. The one I preferred to forget about since I'd nearly been killed by the owner. But I remembered it had been pretty old-fashioned-looking, with lots of dark wallpaper and heavy furniture along the walls of the enormous hallway.

Now the wallpaper had been stripped and the walls painted a light color that really made the long hallway running from the front door to the back seem much bigger. Small side tables with two comfy-looking plush chairs made little islands where people could sit and talk at various places along the walls below antique looking sconces and the still-dark floors gleamed with a high polish where stray beams of sunlight hit them.

Dixie poked me in the ribs. "Let's go. We're not going to be able to see much of anything like this."

I stepped back, casting a glance along the porch. No open blinds in any of the windows. Dixie may be right, but my stubborn streak kicked in right about then. I'd come here to do some peeking and I intended to do it. As we descended the front steps, my attention was caught by movement in the trees out at the edge of the property line.

It was Harley Ann and Bobby, running down through the woods. They must be feeling young love. "Sweet lovers love the spring," according to old Will Shakespeare. I ignored the kids and turned to Dixie.

"Let's go around back first. There might be a window or two back there we can get a gander through."

Dixie sighed deep, but I knew we were heading on

around back.

As we walked, I saw spring bulbs pushing up through the ground in the beautifully mulched beds all around the house. Must be hundreds of little green triangles. Those would be tulips and spring irises at this time of year. And the taller, skinny greens would burst into buttercups soon.

Ha! Miss Edna wasn't the only one in town who knew something about gardening. A big yellow bell bush at the corner of the house already sported buds about to break open. Green leaves had begun popping out on the dead-looking stalks of some big hydrangea bushes around back. They'd be gorgeous in bloom against the white of the stone.

Dixie and I walked up the steps of the not-quite-as-fancy back porch, where some wrought-iron tables and chairs were scattered around. Probably for guests who wanted to sit out here in the evening.

A big pool had been installed on the grounds back here. It was covered right now, but there wasn't any fencing around it. I wondered briefly how the new owners planned to keep the local kids from using it but decided that wasn't my concern. Right now I just wanted to see inside.

""Hey, Dixie. Look!" I pointed to the back door. It wasn't quite closed all the way.

"I don't like this," Dixie said.

"What? It's probably hard to get closed tight. A lot of

these old houses are like that. At least they are if they still have the original doors. My back door is that way. You have to pull the knob up and toward you hard to get it to catch completely. I bet one of the workers didn't get it shut tight. Come on."

Pushing the door open further, I was met with semi murky light. The blinds were all drawn back here too, but I made out high-end commercial appliances in place. The stovetop could definitely handle a lot of food. And with a pang of envy, I noticed a pot filler had been installed. I'd love to have one of those. Even though I didn't cook enough to really justify it. Which was why I hadn't gone to the expense of having one installed in my own home.

Big light-colored cabinets stretched up to the high ceiling. I didn't care for them myself, but they did make this kitchen appear big and amazing. A gorgeous sea-glass-colored backsplash set them off. My eyes wandered the room, admiring all the updated style and picking up on new additions to make it a commercial kitchen rather than a home one. I loved the big island they'd installed. And then I noticed it. A cut glass punchbowl with a cake in it sitting out on the countertop of the island. I turned to Dixie, standing behind me in the doorway.

"Looky there. Someone left a cake out on the counter. I bet it's stale as sawdust by now."

Eyes big as saucers, Dixie pointed a shaking finger

past me to the floor.

Turning, I saw man-sized feet clad in brown loafers, toes pointing upward, sticking out from behind the island. Someone was on the floor on their back on brand-new tile in browns, blues and beige covering the floor. I held my breath. No sounds of breathing or moans of pain. The feet didn't move, so I edged closer.

A hand grabbed my upper arm and I nearly took Dixie out with a left cross when I swung around. She shook her head and motioned back to the door. I shook my head and took a step closer to the island. Her grip tightened on my arm as she pulled her cell phone from her pocket with the other hand.

"I'm callin' Ben," she whispered. "You know he won't want us messing around in here."

I shook off her restraining hand. "Go on and call him," I whispered back. "He needs to get out here. But I'm going to poke around a little before he does." I regretted not having my purse with me. I'd put my house key in the pocket of my jeans before we left for our walk up here. It'd seemed ridiculous to carry a purse out in the woods and along the trails we'd walked. Now that we'd discovered a body, it would have been great to have it. So I could put on the crime scene booties I kept in there so I wouldn't contaminate the evidence.

The right thing to do under the circumstances would

be to leave with Dixie. But, since I couldn't bring myself to do that, I squatted and took off my shoes. My socks should be clean enough not to contaminate the scene. Standing back up, I saw Dixie shaking her head. She knew I wouldn't listen to her. She motioned with her head to the back door. I nodded back and she went out onto the porch, where I heard her talking on her phone.

I didn't know why we were being so quiet. If a killer had been lurking around when we got there, he was long gone now. If the guy on the floor wasn't already dead I felt pretty sure he would have confronted us by now. Or moaned or shifted around at the least. I felt like I knew who was lying there. Miss Edna had told me Luxen Natolovich had been hired as a baker by the new owners. So it seemed a given it was going to be him I'd see when I rounded the island.

I took a deep breath and looked. Yep. That was Luxen all right. Lying in a pool of blood. There was a very small bullet hole in his forehead. No other wounds. I didn't see any signs of a struggle. Which seemed odd. If someone was trying to shoot me between the eyes, I'm pretty sure I was gonna be clawing and fighting like a wildcat. One bright red handprint stained the light-colored cabinet next to him. Like he'd tried to catch himself on the way down.

"Who is it?" Dixie asked from the door, looking like she wanted to run, puke, scream or all three.

"It's Luxen Natolovich," I answered, overcome with a weird sense of calm.

Her eyes bugged out and she retreated to the porch. I heard the agitated sound of her voice and assumed she was talking to Ben. I let my eyes drift upward from the body and saw drips of blood down the cabinet. And, as my eyes focused on the countertop, I realized what I'd initially thought was spilled icing was actually a pool of blood. Ick!

I thought the cake on the counter was a strawberry punch bowl cake, but I saw the red fruit were cherries instead. The cut-glass bowl was incredibly beautiful and looked antique. Hmm. Had he been creating something that would be a specialty at the new Inn? What was up with the cherries instead of the more traditional strawberries?

And, more to the point, how could I be standing there in this totally calm state making these insane observations? Maybe I'd slipped a cog. Or maybe it was all going to hit me later. I heard a hissing sound and looked toward the door. Dixie.

"Lily Gayle. Ben says get out of there and wait for him on the porch."

I frowned. "Why did you tell him I was in the kitchen?"

Dixie snickered. "I didn't. He knew without me saying anything about it."

I lifted each foot to check for blood before I walked

across the kitchen. Clean. Somehow I'd managed to avoid the drips on the floor near the body. I edged back toward the door, stopping on the way to pick up my tennis shoes.

Sitting at one of the little tables outside, I put them back on, and Dixie and I waited in silence for Ben. I was considering how this had happened and who might have done it. I figured Dixie was regretting she'd come with me. But what was done was done.

It wasn't much of a wait before I saw Ben's sheriff's cruiser coming up the drive. No lights. No siren. Driving at a normal pace. Guess he figured since Luxen was already dead there was no sense in rushing around, drawing attention to himself and getting folks wondering where he was going in such a hurry.

He'd been the county sheriff for quite a few years now. Had some good years and some not so good ones. But he was loved by everyone in the county and many was the time he'd rolled up on a scene and stopped arguments with just a look. In addition to being the county sheriff, Ben was my first cousin. And, if I was honest, had saved my bacon on a few occasions when my curiosity had gotten me in some sticky situations.

He got out of the car with a face like a thundercloud and I knew I was in for a big lecture. But seriously, how could I have known there would be a dead body here? This was a purely innocent little adventure. I put on my best innocent smile and waved. He didn't wave back. Or smile. If anything, his eyebrows got even closer together and his frown deeper. Yep. Mad as a wet hen. I straightened my spine and put my shoulders back. Dixie was all hunched up in her chair like a scared kitten. There wouldn't be much defense from that quarter.

CHAPTER FIVE

Just about every woman in town had taken up space in the It'll Grow Back when I walked in the door the day after news of Luxen's murder washed through town like a flood. A person could hardly hear herself think in the din of voices.

Everyone seemed to have heard a rumor about Luxen at some point in her life and was anxious to share it and gain the spotlight, even if only for a short moment. Such was life in a small town. The first to speak was remembered as an expert later.

Taking stock of the faces, I spotted several women I knew usually get their hair done over in Hernando. I glared at them and they looked away. Good. This shop wasn't good enough for them to get their hair done there on a regular basis, but they sure knew where to flock for the latest news.

If it were up to me, I'd be getting them set up for

appointments for the most expensive services offered by the shop before I'd let them take up space in the chairs upfront that rightfully belonged to regular customers who got here early; or maybe just dropping in to share or hear news.

But Dixie wasn't mean like me.

She'd let them sit in there soaking up all the gossip without an appointment for anything—except their conscience, if they had one—just because she's a good egg. I shot several of them the evil eye as I made my way past them and into the heart of the shop, where all the chairs were taken by woman at various stages of hair fixing. Dixie and all three of the part-time hair stylists were as busy as a one-legged man in an ass-kickin' contest.

'Y'all know he wasn't from around here," quavered an elderly voice just as I walked up.

I scanned the occupants of the chairs to see who'd said it. Not surprised when I spotted her.

Mildred's wet hair stuck to her head, emphasizing the big ears she usually kept hidden with carefully styled blue-rinsed locks. Snippets of hair dotted the plastic cape around her shoulders and her pupils were as big as grapes because she didn't have her glasses on. Not a great look for an oracle, but who could control the timing of these things?

The announcement brought near silence to the shop.

Just the outsiders upfront continued to talk, not having heard Mildred. A pronouncement of *not from around here* generally brought this kind of reaction, whether the person was living or dead. Like a queen holding court, Mildred paused, savoring her moment in the sun.

My ears perked up. I'd been born and raised right here and didn't know Luxen hadn't been. Though, now that I really thought about it, he did have a tiny accent that was different from our own. But then, contrary to what people in the rest of the country thought, there were a multitude of southern accents.

Those with a really good ear could tell you exactly where a person had grown up after just one conversation. Not being one of those gifted with that talent, I never consciously noted the nuances of those various accents.

After several moments of silence, and making sure she had the attention of all the regulars, Mildred went on. "That's right. All you youngsters wouldn't know about it. Seems like they don't teach history around here anymore." She shook her head. "Back after the end of World War II, there was a refugee camp over in Tate County. Folks there were from a country called Latvia. Can't say as I know why it got built there. But that's neither here nor there. Luxen's family was one of the ones that lived there. He was just a boy at that time. He came here as a young man."

Excited chatter broke out. This was news! How could we not have known that about someone who'd lived here so long? We knew the histories of every family here. Backward and forward. How had Luxen escaped our scrutiny?

Completely ignoring everyone else in the shop, I edged closer. Dixie put down the hair dryer she's been about to use on Mildred and picked up a roller instead. Couldn't let a customer's hair dry by itself, but we'd never be able to hear these revelations over the sound of the dryer.

As Dixie began winding the wet strands around the first roller, Mildred continued. "I was a not-so-young war widow myself when Luxen came to Mercy." She paused, cleared her throat. Dixie glanced up from the roller, met my eye. We stayed respectfully silent while Mildred pulled herself together.

She'd never gotten over the death of her young husband and never remarried. She'd raised their daughter, born after her daddy was killed, all by herself. My throat closed as I remember my own husband. Gone eight years now, but it still seemed like yesterday. I guessed Mildred and I had that in common. We'd loved only once.

Dixie and I jumped when Mildred cleared her throat. "Anyway. I reckon it was nineteen fifty-three. Or thereabouts. The newspaper ran a big story about him being a refugee and coming here and opening the bakery."

43

I made a mental note to go over to the library to look up the old article on microfilm. I wondered why the information hadn't been included in Luxen's obituary. Alvin Bishop must have been up all night getting the obit ready to make the deadline for today's paper. Come to think of it, it hadn't included the names of any family members. Luxen had been single all his life, so I hadn't registered the lack of family names. I made another mental note to run over to the newspaper office to have a chat with Alvin and his wife, Marlene.

I heard chair legs scraping behind me and turned to see what was going on.

The nonregulars upfront shuffled around, glanced back at us. One of them even had the nerve to raise her hand in a farewell wave as they exited the shop en masse. My blood started a slow simmer. Guess they'd got what they came for. Before the simmer could become a boil, Mildred started talking again and I let it go. For now.

The ladies in the other salon chairs looked like they'd lost interest in the conversation. At least they didn't seem to be paying attention to us.

"I wonder why Miss Edna hasn't mentioned any of this," I said.

"Oh, poo," replied Mildred. "Edna had a—what do the young folks call it these days? Oh, yes, a crush. On Luxen, in the old days."

My mind boggled at the thought of Miss Edna having a crush on someone. It seemed so out of character for the woman I knew. But then, even Miss Edna was young once. And probably had wanted to have a husband and kids.

"He never paid her any attention beyond being friendly…like he was to everybody. But he was a handsome man in his prime, so I can't really blame Edna for trying."

Dixie wound another couple of rollers into Mildred's hair as the three of us contemplated the past, young love, and men in general. I wondered if Miss Edna's own broken heart might be affecting her attitude toward Harley Ann and Bobby. She'd never in a million years admit it if that was the case.

Giving myself a mental shake to clear the cobwebs, I turned to Dixie. "Can you put me on your book for tomorrow to get my roots done?"

"Sure, hon." Her eyes went to the top of my head. "You're a little overdue."

I felt that little silver skunk stripe along my part start glowing like a neon sign. I was going home for a cap before I went anywhere else today.

CHAPTER SIX

"Chocolate gravy?" asked Helen, order pad in hand. She'd been waiting tables at the Grits and Gravy Café for two generation of locals. Today her long black hair was braided and coiled around her head like a Swiss miss and she was dressed in one of the new promo T-shirts for sale at the counter by the cash register, khakis rolled at the ankle and Keds. She was pushing seventy and sprier than I was. And the color of her hair was courtesy of the It'll Grow Back. She had a standing monthly appointment with Dixie.

I smiled. "You know me well."

"Not hard when you have the same thing every time you come in." Helen stuck the order pad in the back pocket of her khakis. "Where's the rest of the gang?"

"They'll be here directly, I'm sure." I leaned back in my chair to wait. Helen wouldn't bring my breakfast until the rest of the gang arrived. A hand appeared over my shoulder holding a tall glass of sweet tea. I could drink my weight in the sweet tea they make here and Helen knows it.

I smiled. "Thanks, Helen."

"Didn't think I'd forgot, did you?"

"You? Never. Your mind is like a steel trap. I don't know who you think you're foolin' with that order pad. You've got us all memorized." I frowned. "Well, that sounds like we're a bunch of old fuddy-duddies. I think I should mix it up a little bit to keep you on your toes."

Helen lifted an eyebrow and pulled the order pad from her pocket.

I laughed. No way was I giving up my chocolate gravy. I never made it myself, so it was my treat whenever I came here. "Maybe next time."

"That's what I thought." Helen put the order pad back in her pocket. "Nothing wrong with knowing what you like."

Sipping my sweet tea, I observed the café.

The Grits and Gravy had been opened by the Simpson family back in 1900. Luckily, there was a child in each generation with the restaurant bug to keep it running. Kyle was the current Simpson to be running it. He was the one who'd changed the name and spruced it up most recently. It had undergone some other changes, updates and renovations over the years but still maintained its small-town charm.

Mismatched wooden chairs with the edges worn smooth from years of use surrounded solid wood tables in a variety of stains, some dark, some light. Red-and-white-gingham curtains added a splash of color to the place while still allowing a view out to the street.

Ole Miss and Mississippi State banners vied with each other on the walls along with picture of famous Mississippi writers like Eudora Welty and William Faulkner, and, most recently, John Grisham and Greg Isles. No TV's adorned the walls. Kyle said his restaurant was for the appreciation of good food and good conversation, not watching the boob tube. Funny, I would have thought he was too young to know that expression. Must have gotten it from his mama and daddy.

I was sitting at our regular table, the big round one smack dab in the middle of the café. We met here for breakfast every Thursday morning. Me, Dixie, Missy Halbert if she didn't have a real estate showing, Pauline from the bank, Miss Edna and, now, Harley Ann.

Outside, the sun shone bright, but across the street Luxen's bakery was dark. The bright neon sign spelling "Luxen's" that he'd been so proud of was unlit. The place appeared old and broken somehow in the bright morning and my heart hurt for the man none of us had truly known.

The door to the café opened, pulling me from my dark

thoughts.

Dixie came, in waving to Helen as she crossed the room. "My regular," she hollered, and Helen rolled her eyes. I burst out laughing.

"What's so funny?" Dixie asked as she pulled out the chair next to me and sat.

"Helen and I were talking about what old farts our group is."

"Old fart? Speak for yourself!"

The door opened again and Miss Edna, accompanied by Harley Ann, entered. Helen gave them a minute to get settled at the table, then came over to get their order. Miss Edna would never shout across the café. And Harley Ann hadn›t established her regular order yet. She was still sampling the menu.

Miss Edna ordered her regular; over medium fried eggs, sausage and biscuits. Dixie and I snickered and I caught a smile on Helen's face. She'd never laugh at Miss Edna.

"What in tarnation is so funny?" Miss Edna asked.

"We've been talking this morning about how all y'all have your special favorites you order every time you come in here," Helen replied.

"Well, I don't see what's wrong with knowing what I want." Miss Edna gave all three of us a sharp look.

"Couldn't agree more, Miss Edna." Helen turned to

Harley Ann. "So, young lady, have you decided what you're trying this visit? Or have you decided what your regular order is going to be?"

Harley Ann grinned. "I)m still sampling. I want to try everything before I settle down."

"A good thought for all parts of your life," said Miss Edna, and I knew she was referring to Bobby Moore. Harley Ann flushed a pretty pink.

"Yes, ma'am," she said to her aunt. "I'm going to have the Mash Up today, Helen."

The Mash Up was a full breakfast with all the items stacked up on top of each other. A waffle, sausage patties, hash browns, diced ham and scrambled eggs. All topped with cheese melted down over it and sprinkled with green onions. In theory, I love it, but in practice I'd never be able to eat all that.

"Could I get some extra biscuits, Helen?" Harley Ann asked.

"Why, sure," Helen answered and headed back to the kitchen to put in the new orders.

Harley Ann reached into her purse and brought out a small Mason jar. My heart skipped a beat. She'd brought some of her butter. As Harley Ann removed the lid, I saw a dark, brownish-red chunky substance.

"This one is a little different." She scooped some onto a teaspoon from the table, passed it to Dixie, and motioned me to give her my own teaspoon. "This is bacon jam instead of butter. I think it's pretty good. Y'all give it a little try now and we'll dig into it later when Helen bring the extra biscuits."

Dixie looked like she was in hog heaven. I took a nibble of the jam and joined her. It was delicious. The absolutely perfect mix of sweet and salty. And something else. I took another nibble. Hmm. Something familiar, but I couldn't quite tease it out. I took one more nibble. Was it…alcohol? I swirled the jam around in my mouth. Yep. It sure was.

I laughed. "Girl, you're gonna end up getting us all tipsy this morning."

Miss Edna smiled. "Good old Tennessee sipping whiskey. I wanted her to use my special recipe punch ingredient, but she says it won't work in the jam."

I nearly choked on my last bite of the jam. Everybody knew Miss Edna's secret ingredient was moonshine. I could understand Harley Ann not wanting to use it in her jam recipe. Who knew? It might blow up or something with that high an alcohol content. But this? Yum!

"Harley Ann, you have got to sell this stuff," Dixie said, licking every little bit of the jam from her spoon. "You'll be rich in no time!"

Harley Ann turned sad eyes to me. I held her gaze for a minute, feeling terrible for her about Luxen being so rude to both of us. And now Luxen was dead, so there was no way we could persuade him to change his mind and give her a chance.

Missy and Pauline arrived together and sat down.

"What›s that y'all are moaning over?" Missy asked, eyeing the container sitting on the table. Which, unfortunately, was now kind of low on contents.

"Y'all give me your spoons." Harley Ann held out her hand and both ladies handed over their spoons. Once they got them back, full of the jam, I noted a little jealously, both took a tentative taste. Then quickly finished off the rest.

"I declare," said Pauline. "I believe that's the best bacon jam I ever ate. My gramma used to make some when I was a little girl, but yours has her beat."

Missy nodded agreement and Harley Ann beamed.

"Too bad Luxen's dead. He could have let you sell this at his bakery," said Pauline. "I know he would have loved to help you out."

Harley Ann and I locked eyes again and Miss Edna cleared her throat.

"Oh my goodness gracious." Pauline put her hands to her face. "That sounded just awful! I'm sorry Luxen's dead at all. I didn›t mean…"

Miss Edna patted her hand. "Don't fret, Pauline. We know what you meant."

The café door opened and three men and a woman entered and stood looking around for a moment. All of us turned our eyes in their direction, observing as they made their way to a table nearby.

The oldest man looked like he'd got one foot in the grave and the other one on a banana peel. He was so hunched over and wizened, I wondered how he managed to walk. The middle one of the men was a younger version of the old guy, but he was no spring chicken himself. Maybe in Miss Edna's age range, late seventyish. The other man must be married to the attractive woman who was with the group. They struck me as being around my own age. Missy raised her hand, waving across to them. The men got an annoyed look on their faces, but the woman briefly raised a hand in acknowledgment.

"They're the new owners of the Midnight Dragonfly," Missy whispered to us. I stared with more interest at the group. They were studying their menus, ignoring us. I felt a small twinge of guilt for having been up there peeping around…and discovering the dead body on their property.

And with that, another thought occurred to me. One that caused the tiny hairs on the back of my neck to stand up. Had they been somewhere in the house when Luxen was murdered? Or even when Dixie and I were nosing around?

"Where are they living, Missy? Not up at the Inn, are

they?" I asked as casually as possible. Dixie paled, and I knew she was tuning in to my thought processes.

Missy rattled on, oblivious to the undercurrents from Dixie and me. "Oh no. Not yet. They're going to live upstairs now that it's finished, but they didn't want to live there while all the renovations were going on. They were renting a place over in Hernando for the past six months."

She glanced in their direction. Probably to see if they were taking note of all the whispering going on at our table. They seemed absorbed in one another.

Missy went on. "You know, I didn't think they were going to buy the old Mitchell place. They were looking at three in different places. And Brenda seemed more interested in the one in Georgia."

Missy shook her head. "Just goes to show you: Don't give up hope. Because they came back for one more look before making their final decision and I toured them through town. I pointed out the bookstore and the ice cream parlor and the bakery. Well, really just everything in town. The two older men seemed to perk up and the next thing I knew, they were signing on the dotted line for Mitchell Manor. And my bank account is in better shape than it's been in a very long time."

"I can't imagine the town would have changed their mind," Miss Edna said. "There's not much to it."

Missy made an offended, huffing sound. 'Why, Miss

Edna. All kinds of wonderful changes have been taking place here. Mercy will be on the map as a destination one of these days. You mark my words."

"I suppose they're Yankees," Miss Edna said with a sniff.

Missy seemed confused, no doubt wondering why Miss Edna was being so mean about the newcomers. "They're from Boston," she admitted. "At least the men are. But they're nice as can be. Well, Charles is," she amended. "Viktor—that's the oldest man—and Sergei—that's the middle one—can be a little difficult. But Brenda is from Virginia. Born and bred. She's the sweetest thing. She's always wanted to have a really nice bed-and-breakfast out in the country. And her husband wanted to indulge her. So that's how they ended up here in Mercy."

Miss Edna did an actual eye roll. A first. "Methuselah over there don't strike me as the type to indulge anybody."

I felt awful for Missy. And curious about the family. Viktor and Sergei? Those were pretty unusual names. Even for Boston, I was thinking. So I got the attention off Miss Edna's fit of pique. "What's their last name?" I asked Missy.

"Smythe," she said.

"Well, didn't that just take the cake? Smythe. Who would ever pair those unusual names with one so common."

Just then, Helen brought out our food. She had it all balanced on a tray as big as she was. Holding it over her head in one hand. I couldn't help but think she was showing off for the newcomers.

And they were watching with awe on their faces. Even the kind of scary oldest guy. I guess if you weren't used to seeing Helen do that balancing act, you would be impressed.

When she arrived at our table she lowered the tray onto the table next to us without missing a beat and placed our food in front of us. I fell to eating my chocolate gravy. It was a marvelous, chocolaty goodness, just the right consistency oozing over hot, homemade buttermilk biscuits. Silence descended over our group, an homage to the excellent cooking here.

After we all finished, Harley Ann pulled another small Mason jar from her purse and passed it around the table with the plate of extra biscuits. We all slathered the chunky bacon jam on the warm biscuits and bit. A collective sigh went up around the table.

Then, like the bad fairy in an old tale, Ben Carter walked through the door and zeroed in on our table.

CHAPTER SEVEN

I strolled down the sidewalk to the small building on the square that housed our local newspaper, *The Argus*, thinking over everything that had just happened. My brain whirled like a dervish with all Ben's questions to our group and the lie that Harley Ann had told.

Why hadn't she admitted she'd been in the woods with Bobby yesterday afternoon? Ben had cut his eyes to me when Harley Ann had said she'd never been out that way. Did he think I'd made it up? My own eyes had gone to Dixie, who appeared to be as confused as I felt.

But both of us kept our mouths shut. No point in saying anything in front of everybody. The whole episode had left me with a bad taste in my mouth.

Then my brain did some more whirling as I wondered what questions, and answers, had happened across the scarred wooden floor of the Grits and Gravy at the Smythe family table. And that last name still grated on my nerves in conjunction with those first names.

The office was in front of me before I realized I'd come this far down the square. The building was one of the oldest in town, built cheek by jowl with all the others on the square.

Having seen what had happened to a lot of squares in small places just like Mercy, I was grateful that all of ours were still standing. They lent so much atmosphere to the town. All two stories high because, back then, the proprietors lived upstairs, the upper floors were now apartments rented out to young couples or to just-getting-started young adults who wanted to live somewhere other than with Mama and Daddy.

I pushed open the glass door into the newspaper office and saw Marlene sitting behind the desk upfront. She and Alvin had run the newspaper for as long as I could remember. He had taken it over from his dad back in the seventies.

""Hey, Marlene. How're you doin'?"

"Doing good, Lily Gayle. I heard you and Dixie were the ones that found poor old Luxen up at the Mitchell place." She pushed her glasses back up her nose, giving me a sympathetic look from big gray eyes.

I didn't detect even one bit of smartassness from Marlene in that comment. But that's Marlene, sweet-natured as the day is long.

58

"Yes, it was us." I shivered unexpectedly. *Goose walking over your grave*, my mama used to say when that happened. I pulled my attention back to Marlene. "I want to take a look at the old newspapers from the mid-Forties. Mildred told me and Dixie that when Luxen first came to town there was a big write-up in *The Argus*."

"Mercy," said Marlene. "That's way back there. And I'm not sure if we have those on microfilm yet." She pushed back from her desk and motioned me toward the back. "We've been putting all the old papers on microfilm for a while, but we started with the very oldest because they were in the worst shape. You wouldn't believe how boring those papers from the eighteen hundreds are. Not much exciting stuff got printed. It was all word of mouth because nobody wanted anything scandalous printed. But it's a genealogist's dream. If you want to know who got born, married or died, you'll find it in there.

But I guess you already know that since you do genealogy researches for people." She pushed open a wooden door at the end of a dark hall, flicked on a light and we entered a small, windowless room with floor-to-ceiling newspapers and a small desk with a setup for microfilm. I sneezed from the old paper smell mixed with dust.

Marlene gave me a sympathetic smile. "I know just how you feel. I can't hardly be back here. It makes my allergies go crazy. Poor Alvin has to do all the work with microfilming because if I try to do it my eyes swell up like a toad frog, and my voice starts sounding like one too."

She was walking along the shelves lining the room and I saw that each shelf had a date written in big black letters along the edge. "As we get them on microfilm, we're sending these down to Jackson to be saved in the archives there. So, believe it or not, this room is nowhere as crowded as it used to be."

She stopped at a shelf with 1945 marked on it "Hmm. I guess we haven't gotten to the nineteen forties yet. Sorry about that. Do you happen to know specifically what year and month you're looking for?"

I thought back to the conversation at Dixie's shop that day. Had Mildred said what year? I struggled to call back the details. Was the camp in Hernando during the war? Or after? And when had she said Luxen came here? Oh. Yes. As a young man. And Miss Edna had had a crush on him. Soooooo. The Fifties?

"Let's start with the early Fifties, now that I think about it. That might be closer to right."

Marlene moved along the shelves and stopped a few feet away. "Here they are. Good thing *The Argus* is a weekly. Not so many to go through." She dusted her hands off on her pants. "I've got to get out of here before my sinuses start acting up. Feel free to look through the

60

papers, and give me a holler if you want to copy anything. I can do that for you upfront." She exited the room, leaving the door open behind her. Probably so I'd have a little ventilation in here.

I didn't like the claustrophobic atmosphere, but needs must when the Devil drives. I chose 1952 at random and pulled the first January edition from the pile. Sitting at the small desk with the not-so-bright light overhead, I began my search.

Thirty minutes later, when I was dusty, thirsty and without results, Marlene popped her head around the door. "Hey, hon. I checked with Al to see if he remembered more about the article you're wanting to find. He said try nineteen fifty-three. He knows the bakery opened the year he was born."

She shook her head. "He can't remember the year we got married or the year Alisha was born, but he can remember the year the bakery opened. Go figure." She disappeared from the doorway as I moved over to the newspaper shelves.

I decided something as big as a displaced person from the war moving to town would have been front-page news. So, instead of paging very carefully through all the brittle pages of old papers, scared to death I was going to damage them, I decided to glance at all the front pages first.

January, nope. February, nope. March, nope. I was starting to wonder if my logic was faulty when I saw a big picture on the front page of the issue from the second week in April of 1953. I laughed a little because Al had remembered correctly.

There was a young Luxen standing in front of the bakery. Mildred was right; he *was* a handsome young man. Even though the photo was black and white you could tell he had a head full of wavy blonde hair. He looked proud as a peacock standing there on the sidewalk on a sunny day long ago. My heart skipped a beat with sadness. No one could have known things would turn out this way.

I read every word of the article. He'd come to the United States in 1949 with his parents. A group of about 100 mostly Latvians who'd been displaced by the war boarded a ship to the United States at the invitation of an American officer from Mississippi who'd met them in Europe while working with displaced persons.

They arrived in Senatobia by train and built a small community there. Even though Luxen's family was considered Czechoslovakian, they'd gotten included with a group of displaced Latvians being sponsored because his mother was Latvian. I did the math and figured out he'd been sixteen then. So when he'd come here to Mercy, he'd been only twenty.

Just as I was leaving the room, my foot caught on

an uneven spot on the old floor. I didn't want to drop or damage the old newspaper, so I tried to keep my upper body still while my feet did an Irish clog dance to regain my balance. I did several squats to top off my dance routine, and just as I thought I was catching my balance, I crashed into the wall and managed to flip the light switch off. But, hey, I was still standing up and the newspaper wasn't hurt.

Score one for me. Hopefully I wouldn't have a giant bruise on my upper arm and shoulder tomorrow. I strolled up the hallway to get Marlene to make me a copy of the story. She was very obviously holding in laughter. Had she been looking down the hall while I was saving the darn newspaper?

"So. You found what you were looking for," she said with only a tiny chuckle. "I'm sorry Al was out of town today and couldn't be here to help you search."

She gave me a once-over and I glanced down. My shirt and the upper thighs of my jeans were covered in dusty smudges. I grimaced. I hadn't realized how filthy I was getting as I searched through the dusty old papers.

Handing her the paper, I asked, "Can you make me a copy of the article?"

She took the paper, placing it carefully on her desk. Then she surprised me by getting out her cell phone and snapping a picture of the article without using the flash.

"We try to avoid bright light on the papers. It deteriorates them, and this helps keep that from happening." She emailed the photo to her computer, then enhanced the picture once it was up on her screen to make it clearer. Then I heard the printer across the room start up.

"There you go." Marlene grinned at me. "Gotta love modern technology. I printed three copies just in case."

"I was wondering if you or Al know anything about the family that bought the Mitchell place. They came in to the Grits and Gravy this morning and Missy pointed them out to us. They seem like an odd group."

Marlene grimaced. "Yeah. The old guy give me the creeps." She shivered. "And the son is pretty weird too. But the grandson and his wife seem really nice."

I nodded. "Missy said they bought the place because the granddaughter-in-law wanted a B-and-B." I brushed uselessly at the smudges on my jeans and sighed, giving up. "I don't remember seeing any articles in the paper about them buying the old place."

Marlene pushed back from her desk. "You're right. There weren't any articles. The creepy guy made it really clear they didn't want any personal attention. Just stuff about the B-and-B." She moved to a file cabinet across the room and opened a drawer. "But they did place an ad for a dessert chef."

She pulled a form from one of the files and brought it

over to me. "I thought it was weird that they wanted to place an ad like that. There was no one around here except Luxen who had the kind of experience they wanted. And they simply could have gone to the bakery and asked him if he wanted to moonlight for them. Take a look at the ad."

I smoothed out the paper and read Marlene's neat script.

Dessert chef needed for soon-to-open bed-and-breakfast
in Mercy. Must have extensive experience. Vatrushki.
Send inquiries to P.O. Box 123, Senatobia, MS 38668

Puzzled, I asked. "What's that last word?"

She shook her head, spreading her hands. "I have no idea. I made him spell it twice so I could be sure I had it right."

"The ad was placed over the phone?"

"Yep. And paid with a credit card. The old guy is hard to understand. He has some kind of odd accent I've never heard before. But that's what they wanted."

I mulled it over. It struck me as really odd that the ad had been placed in our local paper. Because let's face it, the talent pool for that job was nonexistent here. With the exception of Luxen. But maybe they'd been covering all the bases. After all, we're within driving distance of other towns that have nice restaurants. And maybe there was somebody in the county who had a hidden talent or worked in one of those restaurants in Memphis or elsewhere.

Still. It seemed off. I made a mental note to check the Memphis newspaper when I headed over to the library to see if they'd run an ad there. And the other county newspapers. Just to cover all the bases.

I held the paper out to Marlene. "Can you make me a copy of this too?"

"Sure." She walked over to the copier, punched some buttons and handed me the copy of the ad placement request and copies of the newspaper article.

'Marlene, you're a doll."

"I know." She smiled. "Thanks for the entertainment," she added and waved as I exited the office.

With my shoulders hunched up around my ears in embarrassment, I tucked the papers into the oversized tote I'd brought with me this morning and walked quickly around the square and down a side street to the library. I intended to get on the internet there to see what else I could find out about the refugee camp in Tate County.

I could do it on my home computer, but I might need to use some other reference material that was only going to be at the library. I just hoped I didn't have to do major battle with Miss Jamerson while I was there. She and I weren't the best of friends. Try as I might to do the right thing, somehow I managed to upset her every time I went in there.

CHAPTER EIGHT

As soon as I walked in, Miss Jamerson gave me the no-nonsense look. And I hadn't even sat down yet. It was rough when people assumed you were a hoodlum. I'm pretty sure that's how Miss Jamerson would classify me. Even though I'm quiet and follow the rules—most of the time. I guess it was those rare occasions I went outside the lines that tipped the balance out of favor for me.

Taking my life in my hands, I ignored the basilisk stare and walked to the information desk. It was just a little gratifying to see the surprised expression in her eyes before she masked it with one of calm indifference. Hard to believe this was the same woman who all the local kids loved for doing the voices when reading at children's hour. I needed to come in sometime and hide in the stacks to hear it for myself. But today, I had another agenda.

"Hey, Miss Jamerson. How're you doin' today?"

"Why, I'm fine as can be, Lily Gayle. What are you

lookin' for today?" She smiled at me.

Well, this was a surprise. I'd better get my information while the gettin' was good. I leaned on the counter just a bit, creating a more private atmosphere, like the two of us were sharing secrets. It seemed to work; she leaned in toward me a little from her side.

"I'm looking for some information about a refugee camp over in Tate County back in the late Forties."

She seemed strangely excited. I had no idea what that was about. It was a really scary look on her, though. I expected her nose to start quivering any minute.

"You're investigating what happened to Luxen, aren't you?" she said. "He came here from that camp."

Well. Well. Well. Wasn't this a turn up? Miss Jamerson knew about Luxen too. But surely she was too young to have had a crush on Luxen herself. I mean, she seemed old as dirt, but she was still working here at the library. They had some kind of mandatory retirement age. Didn't they? She must have been a little girl at the time. Then I realized all the town folk in a certain age group must remember this about Luxen.

"I'm looking up some information to help the sheriff," I said.

Her lips pressed together like she was holding something in. Probably a mean comment about me being a nosy Nellie using locating information for Ben as a cover. She must want something from me, but I couldn't figure out what it could be.

"Do you remember when Luxen first came to Mercy?"

Miss Jamerson's cheeks pinked up and a quick sparkle came into her eyes. Oh my goodness gracious. Miss Jamerson must have been a pretty young girl once upon a time. Bless her heart.

"He was a fine young man. Always a kind word for everyone." Miss Jamerson blushed, and I wondered if he'd had some kind words for her somewhere along the line. "Such an enterprising man. Starting the bakery and settling in like he did. Why, before you knew it, he'd become part of the town. What a pity he never married." Her eyes took on a far away look. "Of course I was far too young for him myself."

She'd said the last with a pained expression. Confirmation of my thoughts about her personal feelings, but nothing about Luxen's. She'd been sweet on Luxen and she hadn't been at the top of his list. But then, it seemed like Miss Edna hadn't been either. "Why do you think he never married?" I asked.

Miss Jamerson frowned. "I don't rightly know, to tell you the truth. Like I said, he was friendly to everyone, but no one comes to mind that he ever seemed to be sweet on."

"You don't remember anything about him and Miss

Edna?" I asked casually.

She drummed her fingers lightly on the big information counter and I stayed quiet, hoping something would occur to her that might shed light on the mystery of a fine-looking man like Luxen staying single his whole life. Miss Jamerson shook her head.

"No. Not Miss Edna. No one. How sad."

She was a bit younger than Miss Edna and Mildred, so anything of that nature might have flew over her head as a young girl. And Miss Edna certainly doesn't make it easy for anyone to know something so personal about her. Even as a young woman I'd bet.

Well shoot. This was getting me nowhere. I glanced around the room and saw a few people I knew from around town scattered here and there in the stacks. And one young girl I thought might be a Hanson from the look of her, staring into one of the computer screens.

Not many people hanging around on a Saturday morning. But in the past few years it seemed like fewer and fewer people spent much time in here. I guess it had become too easy to get books and news on a smartphone or home computer. Sad really.

I took a deep breath of library air, that instantly recognizable scent of old books layered with dust particles floating in sunbeams shining through hot windows that I would know if I were blindfolded. A beloved scent from all through my life. Miss Jamerson cleared her throat with a low, coughing sound, startling me.

"Sorry. Got a little off track there," I said.

She actually smiled at me. Like she knew the thoughts swirling through my head. And maybe she did. She'd been here her whole life and had seen a couple of generations of locals grow up as she stood behind this old desk.

"I came by to see if you have copies of the old newspapers from the surrounding counties on microfilm here." I paused, remembering how mad she'd been at me last time I was in here reading microfilm. I'd left a whole spool threaded on the machine after I'd had words with Alexander Mitchell about my researching his family history.

Now she wasn't batting an eye at the idea of me looking at microfilm. So maybe she was pretty interested in the research herself. Or maybe she was just feeling sentimental about things. Either way, I wasn't looking a gift horse in the mouth. "I want to see what I can find out about that refugee camp back in the late Forties over in Tate County."

She bustled out from behind the counter, heading toward the cabinets holding the microfilm. Uh-oh. Maybe she was planning on handling the films herself. But, thinking it over, that was fine with me.

"You're in luck," she said over her shoulder in a low

voice. "When we first got the microfilm system, one of the Luckett girls was crazy about it and took to it right off. She spent hours getting all the old papers on film. So we just need to pull the rolls from that time frame and take a look."

I wasn't liking this *we* business. Did she plan to stand over me the whole time? I needed that like I needed a hole in my head. Not that anything I was doing was secret, but I really hated it when anyone hovered over me.

She stopped in front of a brown metal cabinet in a row of brown metal cabinets. In a small slot on the front there was a piece of cardboard with *Area Newspapers* and the dates *1945 to 1950* handwritten in a flowing script. Miss Jamerson pulled open a drawer, ran her fingers across the boxes inside and pulled one out. "I looked at the microfilm right after I heard about Luxen. The camp was first started in nineteen forty-nine. Most all of the people there were Latvian, but, if memory serves, there were a handful from other countries close to Latvia as well. They'd all been displaced by the war."

As she pulled out the correct box she added, "Speaking of foreigners living around here. Sergei Smythe was in here yesterday. He was getting a library card. They'll be living up at the B-and-B full time after the grand opening. Said he didn't hold with all this online reading and nothing was quite as satisfying as holding an actual book."

"I have to say I agree wholeheartedly with that sentiment." She opened the box and pulled out a reel, and shreds of microfilm floated to the floor in a scatter of shiny brown confetti.

"I swear I had nothing to do with that," I said as soon as I realized what was going on.

"What in the Sam Hill?" Miss Jamerson said. And, for her, those words were cussin'.

CHAPTER NINE

On Wednesday afternoon, I was still running everything from the weekend through my head. The weird family that now owned the old Mitchell place. All the destroyed microfilm from 1949. Miss Jamerson and I had checked the ones from before and after that date and they were all fine. She couldn't remember anyone pulling microfilm in the last couple of days and didn't know why someone might have destroyed that particular box of film.

She'd been pretty traumatized by the ruin, making all kinds of accusations about teenage hoodlums and filing charges. It'd taken me quite a while to get her calmed down. All the while wondering why that particular film box had been turned into mincemeat. We could have discussed it till the cows came home and still had no answers. I bet she had Todd from the sheriff's department over there right after I left.

The music from "Chattanooga Choo Choo" alerted me

to a call from Miss Edna on my cell phone. She loved Glenn Miller. Taking straight pins out of my mouth, I jabbed them into my pincushion, creaked up from my kneeling position on the floor by the Civil War gown on my mannequin, rushed over to the side table and grabbed the phone before it rolled to voice mail.

Miss Edna didn't even give me a chance to say anything. She was talking a dime a dozen and I wondered if she thought she was leaving me a voice mail.

"Ben Carter was just over here, throwing his weight around and upsetting me and Harley Ann about some things from the past that don't amount to a hill of beans."

I interrupted her barrage of words. "What in the world are you talking about?"

"You come on over here and we'll talk it over. I'm not letting Ben Carter railroad my niece."

The call disconnected and I sat for a minute, trying to digest what she'd said. Ben railroading Harley Ann? It must be about the lie she'd told at the café. That didn't seem like railroad material, though. I ticked over everything I could think of about the girl. Which was precious little, now that I thought about it. There was that whole mysterious past everyone wondered about.

With a sigh, I glanced at the dress I'd been working on all morning and decided I was at a good stopping point. Standing up, I brushed loose snips of thread from my jeans, put on my shoes and headed out the door.

A strong wind blew my hair around as I peddled my bicycle over to Miss Edna's. I should have put on a cap or put my hair in a ponytail before setting out. I hadn't realized there'd been a weather change since early that morning.

Big gray rain clouds scudded across the sky and I regretted not driving a car anymore. I might be in for a wet ride home later on. As I rolled up Miss Edna's front walk, I felt the first drops against my face.

"You need to get over that fear of driving," Miss Edna called from her rocker on the porch. Her words stung me into a reply I knew my mama would wash my mouth out with soap for making.

"You don't drive either. So why are you worried about me?"

Miss Edna's brows drew together. "Don't you sass me, girl. Your mama raised you better."

I steamed quietly because she was right. My mama *did* raise me better. I hadn't driven since my husband died in a car accident eight years before. That was a long time.

And, deep down, I knew she was right. But those were thoughts for another time. Pushing them aside, I climbed the steps and plopped down in the rocker next to her. We sat in silence for a few minutes while my hackles smoothed back down. She didn't mean any harm.

"I'm from a different generation, Lily Gayle," Miss Edna offered. "Women didn't drive much when I was young and I'm too old and nearsighted for it now. But it makes me right angry that a smart, independent woman like you is acting this way about driving. You weren't even in the car when the accident happened."

I squirmed inside. She was right. And I knew it. And she wasn't the only one who thought that way. Ben and Dixie had been exasperated with me all this time too. I shook off those thoughts for now. Time to redirect her attention.

"What did Ben say that's got you in such a tizzy?"

Miss Edna narrowed her eyes. She knew I was changing the subject on her. But I wanted to get on to the one that had brought me over there.

"He came over here this morning making all kinds of insinuations about Harley Ann and that murder up at the Inn. Said he came here instead of making us come to the police station as a courtesy to me. Courtesy my rear end! Wasn't nothing courteous about him this morning." She pounded her cane against the porch boards in emphasis.

"What did he say specifically?" I asked.

"Hmph! He said he'd heard Harley Ann was seen running in the woods around the time of Luxen's body being discovered."

She glared at me, and it took all I had in me not to

cringe. I *was* the one who'd mentioned I'd seen Harley Ann and Bobby in the woods that day. But I surely didn't mean to imply that she'd been involved in the murder. I'd thought maybe they had seen something that might help Ben solve the crime.

"Now, Miss Edna," I began in my own defense, "you know I didn't in a million years mean to get Harley Ann in trouble with Ben."

Miss Edna sniffed. "Well, you did. Now he thinks the girl may have been involved."

What? That was a big jump in thinking. From being seen in an area where she might have a perfectly innocent reason for being to implying she was involved in the crime. Something was definitely missing from this recipe.

"Why did she lie to Ben about being in the woods that day? I'm sure that got his dander up. But he must have something other than me seeing her in the woods to think she might be involved. Is there something you're holding back on me?"

Miss Edna pinched her lips together so tight they turned white, and her grip on the cane turned her knuckles a matching shade. Bingo. There *was* something damning. I waited for her to spill it as the raindrops falling beyond the porch filled the silence.

Like water bursting from a dam, the information popped out of Miss Edna. "She had her own reasons for lying about being in the woods. How could she know you'd already ratted her out?" Miss Edna glared. "He ran a criminal background check on Harley Ann. How dare he!"

Silence descended after the outburst, and I felt like it might be in my best interests if I stayed quiet. But my mind raced right along. I was about to find out why Harley Ann really came to Mercy.

The silence finally stretched to the breaking point and Miss Edna went on. "The girl came here to get a fresh start. And now this mess will be all over town."

Knowing Miss Edna's abhorrence at being the topic of common gossip—even though she didn't mind spreading it at times—I knew how hard it was for her to tell me this story.

"You have my solemn word," I said, "that nothing you tell me will be repeated to anyone." I stared her straight in the eye. "Anyone."

Miss Edna sighed. "I appreciate how hard that would be for you. And I appreciate the thought. But I expect it will get out anyway. And I know you didn't mean to get my girl in trouble."

"Well, why don't you go ahead and tell me, so I get the correct version? You didn't call me over here just to rant about Ben, did you?"

Miss Enda drummed her fingers on the arms of her

rocker. "Harley Ann spent a few years in prison before she came to Mercy."

Shocked, I drew in a sharp breath. Of all the things I'd imagined—and there had been a lot—this wasn't on the list. What could she have done to merit a prison sentence? She seemed so quiet and shy, I found it hard to picture her as a hardened criminal.

"She spent three years in a federal women's prison in Georgia because she was convicted of driving the getaway car in a murder case."

Stunned, I sat back in my rocker. Now I understood why Ben had wanted to question the girl. What a coincidence that someone was murdered in this sleepy little town so soon after her arrival. So, was that shy, self-conscious girl a façade hiding a murderous heart?

As though reading my mind, Miss Edna continued. "I'm not in my dotage and I haven't taken a snake to my bosom."

I opened my mouth to deny it, but she cut me off. "Don't you deny it. I can see on your face that's what you're thinking."

I cleared my throat and said, "I don't think you're in your dotage. I reckon you're about as sharp as anybody I know. But. Well. I mean. Are you sure you aren't being fooled? You never knew her before last year. And then a murder happens here—"

"I thought you liked the girl, Lily Gayle. You went to all the trouble of trying to get Luxen to give her a chance at his bakery."

"I did like her." I paused, considering my next words. I knew they were going to hurt, but I had to say them. Close friends said the hard things to each other, didn't they? "This is a lot to take in, Miss Edna. Luxen ending up dead right after he refused to help her out with her new business. And she lied to Ben about being in the woods that day."

Miss Edna stood up, so much righteous wrath streaming off her, I could nearly see it in the air between us. "Get off my porch, Lily Gayle Lambert."

What? She was throwing me out over a girl she didn't even know a year ago? After all we'd been through together? After she'd known *me* my whole life? I sat frozen in the rocker.

"Go on. You heard me." She made shooing motions with her cane. "I thought I could count on you to help me defend her, but I see you're too narrow-minded after all."

I stood, indignation rising in me. "If you won't give me a minute to be surprised and do some talking out loud, I guess I will go on home. Maybe I shouldn't have said all that out loud. And I'm sorry you're upset. I can see it would be a waste of time to try to talk to you now, so I'll do as you say."

I ran down the rain-slick steps, and by the grace of God, got to the walk without busting my rear. I mounted my bike with my hair streaming water and rode off without looking back.

As I pedaled away in the rain, I felt her eyes boring right into my back. My stomach roiled from the argument. I'd never been good at fighting with the people I loved. Except for Ben. We'd fought like cats and dogs our entire lives, so it was just part of our cousinship.

Thinking about Ben brought me back to Harley Ann and her prison sentence. As I rolled up my drive and into my carport, my mind was filled with useless speculation. And regret. Lots of regret.

I grabbed a big, fluffy towel from the mudroom just inside the back entrance and, toweling my dripping hair, headed upstairs to get some dry clothes. I'd have to meet up with Ben and find out more details. If I could get him to tell me. He might try to pull that ongoing-investigation and need-to-know crap on me like he usually did.

CHAPTER TEN

I'd just gotten out of a good hot shower to shake off the chill of getting wet in the rain and had a towel over my head, drying my hair, when the doorbell rang. Dang it! Who could that be?

I peeped out the window overlooking the front yard but didn't see a car. That didn't necessarily mean anything, though. Whoever it was could have parked close enough to the house for the sweep of the roof on the first floor to block my ability to see their car.

I whipped a comb through my damp hair and glanced in the mirror. Ick. Not the best look for me. But it would have to do. Leaving it loose around my shoulders, I went downstairs. Peeping through the frosted side glass by the front door, I saw Bobby Moore out on the porch.

At least that was who it looked like. The frosted glass distorted everything, and every now and then I got a little bit of a surprise when I opened the door to somebody other than who I thought was out there. Luckily, it has always been somebody I know instead of some stranger wandering around, like a kidnapper or a murderer or something. But those things only happened on TV and in books. Right?

Shaking back my damp curls, I opened the door with the chain on so I could talk to the boy. I wasn't really sure why I left the chain on. It wasn't something I usually did. Maybe I was spooked by the whole Harley-Ann-in-prison surprise. And she'd been running with Bobby lately. Maybe I was turning into a suspicious old woman. Nope. Nope. No way. I straightened my back, standing to my full five feet five inches.

"Hey, Bobby Moore. What brings you here on this rainy afternoon?"

As he raised his eyes to mine, I saw they were red. Like he'd been crying. Uh-oh. What could make Bobby Moore cry?

"Miss Lilly Gayle, you've got to help me. My mama's missing!"

I shut the door, pulled the safety chain, opened it again and he practically fell into my arms in his haste to come in. We sit in the front room. He was tense as a room full of rattlers, and I wasn't sure if he wasn't as dangerous. Him showing up like this was something I never would have imagined.

"All right, Bobby. Calm down and tell me what's going on."

He was sheet white sitting there on the love seat, running shaking hands through his dark hair. "I was talking to her about what was going on with Harley Ann." He shifted his gaze to me to see if I was in on what he was talking about. I nodded and he went on. "I told her about how Sheriff Carter went over to Miss Edna's to question Harley Ann on account of her being in prison before she came here."

His knees started to jiggling and I moved to the love seat next to him and put a hand on his arm. "Calm down, hon."

His big brown eyes beseeched me. "I swear, Miss Lilly Gayle, I don't know what's been happening around here lately. It's like we've landed in some crazy alternate reality."

"Come on, Bobby. Let's go on back to the kitchen. I'm going to fix you some hot, sweet tea. That's the best thing for shock. You look like you've had one." I stood and motioned him to follow me. "Once we get some tea down you, you'll feel better."

I felt like I was luring a green broke stallion down the hall, but my mama swore by hot, sweet tea to get yourself under control and I knew it always worked for me. Hopefully, it would work for Bobby too.

We got to the kitchen and he sat at the big round table by the window as I got my tea kettle out, filled it with water and put it on to boil. While we waited, I sat at the table with him. Just the walk back here seemed to have calmed him a little.

"Now. I've known your mama all my life," I said in a soothing tone of voice. "Why, we went to school together. Did you know that? She stayed to herself a lot, but everybody liked her. And such an unusual name. Rikki. I always thought it was right interesting. I never knew anybody with that name but her." I saw him calming more and more as I spoke.

"I've always thought maybe it was an old family name or something. Even in my genealogy research I never saw anyone else with that name though." I kept up the chatter to fill the space between us for a few minutes. Finally, that old teakettle sang out and I fixed him the hot tea with lots of sugar. I put it down in front of him and he picked up the thick mug and blew across the top.

I sat back down across from him. After he'd taken a few sips, I decided we could get back to business. "I'm sure there's just a misunderstanding of some kind going on here. So, let's figure it out together. You take your time and tell me what's going on. You were talking to your mama about Harley Ann," I remind him.

"Yes'm. And she starts asking me all kinds of questions

about Harley Ann and what she did that got her in prison and why am I going around with her when I know all that about her." He huffed out a breath. "I felt just like a little boy again, getting into trouble with her like that. After I explained everything I knew, she got a weird look on her face and told me there was something she had to do and not to worry." His teacup rattled on the table in his shaking hand and he let go of it. "That was yesterday and I haven't seen her since. She's never been out all night in my whole life."

He sipped the tea carefully, appearing lost in thought. "I've looked everywhere I can think of, but she's nowhere. Then I thought about how good you are with figuring things out and here I am."

I reached across the table and put my hand on his. "We need to go to the sheriff, Bobby. If your mama's been gone since yesterday with no word, he needs to know about it."

Bobby rared back in his chair. "No, ma'am, Miss Lily Gayle. I don't want to go to the sheriff."

Puzzled by his reaction, I asked, "Why not? He's the best one to find your mama."

Bobby got a mulish expression on his face. "I'm not going to the sheriff and that's that. He's already tryin' to railroad Harley Ann about Luxen. I don't want him thinking she did something to my mama. If you won't help me, I'll just keep looking by myself. Or maybe

Harley Ann will help. But she doesn't know the county like you do. Or the people." He stood up. "Thank you for listening and for the tea."

My heart went out to him. Poor thing. I could sort of understand why he was so set against going to Ben and I couldn't let him walk out of here by himself. "Wait, Bobby. I'll help you look if you'll agree to a deal."

I saw wariness in his eyes. "What kind of deal?" he asked.

"If we don't find your mama by dark, we go to Sheriff Carter." I could see he was about to repeat his previous opinion about that and cut him off. "I'm not kidding, Bobby. This is a job for Ben, but I'm willing to compromise just a little at this point. But I can assure you that if your mama's hurt we're both going to regret not going straight to the sheriff."

He looked scared, and a little uncertain. But then his lips firmed up and I knew the moment of weakness was gone. I wished he'd tell me what he had on his mind. Because I knew there was something he hadn't told me. Maybe I could worm it out of him while we were searching. I locked the door behind us and we headed out.

"Where have you already checked?" I asked.

"She's not at the house and I've been to the library, the grocery store, the drug store. Pretty much all over town. So now I don't know where else to go." He gave me a look of hope. "Do you?"

I didn't want to tell him I was stumped. If she wasn't at any of the businesses in town, I didn't really know where to start. There was a rundown motel out on the edge of town, but I sure didn't want to suggest we get anywhere near that place. It was known as a no-tell motel and I was sure he'd be mad as a hornet if I suggested we go out there. I couldn't imagine Rikki would be out there, but then, I couldn't imagine where she'd gotten off to. There weren't many places people could just disappear around here.

We spent a couple of hours riding the back roads in his car, stopping every now and then to scan the woods or pastures. We stopped by the Lickety Split, where locals bought their beer and gas. I stayed in the car and let Bobby go on in by himself to check around. My heart was still hurtin' over the fight with Miss Edna and I just wanted to go home and lick my wounds in private while I figured out how to mend the rift. Personally, I thought this search was a total waste of time. But Rikki Moore wasn't the type to just run off, so where could she be?

"She didn't say a word to you about where she might be going before she disappeared?" I asked Bobby when he got back in the car.

"No, ma'am." Bobby's eyes were steady, scanning the road.

"What did she say to you before she left the house?"

He cut his eyes to me. "I wasn't home when she left. And she didn't leave a note."

So, wherever she was, she didn't mean to be gone long enough to feel the need to leave her son a note. I wanted to scream with frustration. There was absolutely no clue for where to look. I stared out the window on my side of the car in a fruitless attempt to spot her.

Since Bobby hadn't been home when his mama left, we didn't even know what she was wearing and couldn't be trying to spot a color of some kind off in the trees or across a pond. I gulped. Or even *in* a pond. I shook my head to get rid of that thought. There wasn't a single reason to suspect foul play. But it was odd that she'd been gone so long without word. Overnight, to boot.

"So the last conversation you had with her was about Harley Ann?"

He nodded.

Hmm. Not helping. "She didn't give you any hint of what it was about when she said she had some things to take care of?"

"No, ma'am." He shrugged.

"What, specifically, were you saying about Harley Ann?"

"Just that Sheriff Carter thought she might have been involved in what happened to Mr. Luxen on account of her being involved in a murder once before. And that I think Sheriff Carter is full of crap, begging your pardon, Miss Lily Gayle."

I nodded and smiled while I thought over what he'd. Rikki hadn't gone to Ben or Bobby would already know about it. So, what part of the story had gotten her attention to the point that she had something to go take care of? And what on earth could it be?

We kept on meandering around the back roads with no results and I couldn't help but think I wasn't being a lick of help in finding his mother. But maybe he just wanted someone with him. I knew it was easier to deal with things if you didn't feel like you were all alone.

The Midnight Dragonfly loomed up ahead and Bobby slowed the car a bit.

"Do you think your mom went up there?"

He jumped a bit, like I'd startled him. "Oh. No, ma'am. But seeing the place reminded me of something she told me the other day. She said the older men in the family were from Russia."

"Russia? How would she know that? Missy Halbert said they were from Boston."

"I don't know. But she was pretty upset about it. And when I tried to ask more questions she told me to mind my own business." He looks aggrieved. "And she was the one that brought the whole thing up to start with."

I remembered Marlene talking about how hard it had been to understand the old guy on the phone when he'd called in the ad for the dessert chef. Could Rikki know something about the new owners? Maybe something they didn't want spread around? But she'd been born and raised right here in Mercy, so how could she know anything about the new owners? My thoughts swirled in such a tangle I started getting a headache.

"Bobby. It's time to go to the sheriff. We're not gonna find your mama riding around out here like this, and you said you'd already been everywhere in town."

With a deep sigh, Bobby did a three-point turn on the dusty road and we headed back to town.

CHAPTER ELEVEN

We rolled along the dusty back road without talking. At this point there wasn't much to say. Rikki Moore was missing and neither one of us had any idea what to do. So we'd let the long arm of the law handle it.

I couldn't believe I was thinking that way. I was all gung ho on figuring out what had happened to Luxen, but I was shooting blanks on Bobby's mom. I mean seriously, what kind of mama takes off and leaves her baby alone and worried about her?

Bad. Bad. Bad. If I was being honest with myself, I had to admit I was all out of ideas. I bet if I had one, I'd be running it down so fast poor old Bobby's head would spin and he'd never see me for the dust.

As Bobby pulled into the parking lot at the sheriff's department, the sun was slanting low on the horizon, shining right in our eyes as we headed up the walk. Even though it was spring, the temperature had dropped since we'd left my house and I shivered a bit. There was a little bit of a bite to the wind. Beside me, Bobby's feet dragged. I couldn't help feeling sorry for him.

When we walked in the door, Reenie greeted us with a holler. "Hey, Lily Gayle! Hey, Bobby. How's your mama n'em?"

Oh, Lord. I really wished she hadn't said it. And, just like that, Bobby Moore lost his grip right there in the station house. Big tears ran down his cheeks like rain. Reenie gave me a horrified look. As she pushed her ancient rolling chair back from her desk, the most hideous racket came from the old wheels, but Reenie didn't miss a lick. She rushed to Bobby, clucking like a hen with one chick, and put her arm around him.

"Oh, honey. You come on over here and sit." She led him to the visitor chair next to her desk, pulled some tissues from the box on her desk and pushed them into his hand. He crushed the tissues against his eyes, gulping back sobs, and I knew he was about to die from the shame of crying in public like this, so I stepped behind him, put my hand on his shoulder and signaled Reenie with my eyes.

She nodded back at me, visibly holding back her curiosity. I glanced past her and saw Ben standing in the now-open door to his office. The squealing wheels must have brought him out of hibernation. He took in all three of us with a glance, then motioned with his head for me to come in.

I eased past Reenie and Bobby and into Ben's office. He stood in the doorway for a minute, then closed the door. I knew Reenie would get Bobby calmed down and then bring him into the office.

Ben motioned me to sit as he rounded the desk to his own chair. It creaked a bit, like old leather, as he sat down. He probably should replace it, but I didn't see that happening until it actually fell apart and he had no choice. Ben's wasn't one to spend limited department funds on something for himself. He leaned his elbows on the desk and fixed me with his sternest look.

"So, Lily Gayle, what mess have you gotten into this time?"

I drew myself up in the chair. "Now, Ben, there's no reason to be insulting. This is a bad deal." I gave him my best hold-your-horses look. "Bobby cane out to my house earlier today to ask me to help him find his mama."

Ben's eyebrows went up toward his hairline, but he didn't say anything, so I went on.

"I told him *right off* he should come straight to you, but he wouldn't hear of it. So, I agreed to ride around with him and do some searching if he agreed to come here at dark."

Ben started frowning, but he was still keeping quiet, so

I kept going.

"Reenie asked him how's his mama n'em the minute we walked in the door and he just broke down cryin'. Poor thing."

Ben sighed. "I'm not going to lecture you because I know you know better and I don't want to waste more time beating a dead horse." As I opened my mouth to protest, he held up a hand. "I know you said you told him to come on over here. I heard every word you said."

I winced. He was right. And I know it and knew it when I went riding round with Bobby for a few wasted hours. Hours I hoped to goodness hadn't allowed something terrible to happen to his mama.

But in my own defense, I don't believe Bobby would have come to Ben sooner even if I had refused his request for help. I didn't bring this up to Ben because I didn't want to trigger the lecture he said he was goin' to hold back.

"What did the boy tell you happened? Did they have an argument? Anything going on in Rikki's life that would lead her to up and leave or that seemed suspicious?"

I repeated everything Bobby had told me. Straight up and without any embellishments of my own thoughts and opinions. Yet. I'd get to those later, after he'd talked to Bobby.

When I was done talking, Ben went to his door, opened

it a bit and poked his head out. Everything must have calmed down out there because he stepped on out the door and I heard him talking to Reenie and Bobby for a minute; then he and Bobby came into the office.

Bobby was pale as a ghost and his eyes red as fire, but he'd gotten himself under control. Hopefully, he could hang on long enough to tell Ben everything that had happened.

Ben didn't ask me to leave the room, so I kept my seat and Bobby sat in the other visitor chair. He reached out and clasped my hand. Startled, I looked over at his face and saw that for all he was twenty-one, he was still a scared boy who'd lost his mama.

I squeezed his hand and gave him a reassuring smile. Ben sat across from us in the creaky chair, shuffled some folders around, removed a yellow legal pad from under them and turned his attention to Bobby.

"Now, son, how about you tell me everything that's happened?"

Bobby took a deep breath and began. ""Well, Sheriff. I came home from spending time with Harley Ann—you know, Miss Edna's niece?" Ben nodded. "And the house was empty. I didn't think much of it right off because Mama goes to see friends or to get her hair done or to the grocery store. I figured she must be doing something like that." He ran the hand not clutching mine through his hair, leaving it standing on end. "

"But when it got to be dusk and she still wasn't home, I got worried. I called her cell phone but it rolled right on over to voice mail. I left her a message to please call and let me know where she was at, but I didn't hear anything back from her."

His knee began jiggling up and down and I knew he was having trouble keeping a grip on his emotions. "Then, this morning, I started making the rounds of places in town to see if anybody had seen her. But no one had. I was at the end of my rope, so I thought about how good Miss Lily Gayle is about figuring stuff out and I went on out to her place to ask her to look around with me. She wanted to come straight here, but I wouldn't do it."

A guilty rush of triumph flashed through me at his admission that I'd tried to get him to come here right away. Then I gave myself a mental slap. That didn't matter a bitty bit right now. What mattered now was figuring out what had happened to Rikki Moore.

Ben sat back looking thoughtful for a minute, then said, "You sure you don't know what she meant about business she had to take care of?"

Bobby shook his head.

Ben thought some more, his shifting weight causing his old chair to squeak. He leaned back forward putting his forearms on the desk. "Go back over what was said

98

in the conversation between the two of you about the business she had to take care of. Think carefully and try to remember exactly the words she used."

"Do you think it has something to do with why she didn't come home?" Bobby asked.

"We don't have much of anything else to go on at this point." Replied Ben. "So that's where I'm going to start."

Bobby repeated his story with Ben asking questions to clarify. When Bobby got to the part about his mama getting upset about the situation with Harley Ann, Ben interrupted.

"Do you think she was upset more about Harley Ann being in prison or about me questioning her after the murder of Luxen?"

"I....I'm not sure." Bobby stuttered. "She was for sure on a tear about it." He sat quietly for a minute. "But, now that you ask that question, I think maybe she was more upset about you questioning Harley Ann. But that doesn't make any sense. What would she have to do that was connected with that?"

I turned it all over in my mind looking for some connection, but nothing presented itself. Then, I remembered something else Bobby has said while we were riding around.

"Bobby, you said your mama told you the other day that the new owners of the Mitchell place are Russian.

But you didn't know how she knew that. Or why she told you."

"Yes'm" Bobby replied, looking puzzled.

Ben grabbed onto the information. "I wonder if your mama had some kind of contact with them and that's how she knew they are Russian?"

Bobby shrugged. "I don't know when that could have been."

Ben leaned back in his big chair again. "They *are* from Russia. At least the two older ones are." He paused. "When I talked to them after the murder, Viktor told me that he and Sergei had immigrated the United States after the end of World War II. He said they had lost everything and needed a new start. The grandson was born here."

"So how did Rikki know about them?" I wondered.

"That's a good question." Ben stood up. "I'm going up to drive over to Hernando and have a talk with them."

Bobby and I left the station. He dropped me at home and nothing I could say would convince him to stay at my house and sleep in a guest room. He was worried his mama might come home and be wouldn't be there. I watched the tail lights of his car glow down the road as he drove away.

CHAPTER TWELVE

I was awakened early the next morning by someone pounding on my front door like the hounds of hell were after them. Groggily, I looked at the clock on my nightstand. 8 A.M. I'd tossed and turned most of the night. Only falling asleep as dawn streaked the sky. I couldn't get my mind off Bobby and his mama. Struggling into my robe, I rushed down the stairs and jerked open the door. Dixie flashed me a grim look and said, "Get in the car. I'm done with this nonsense."

"Have you lost your ever-lovin' mind?" I clutched my robe closed with one hand and tried to shut the door with the other one.

But Dixie was having none of it. She jammed her size eight foot into the space before I could get the door completely shut, then commenced to pushing from outside while I pushed from inside.

It wasn't clear for a few minutes who was going to

win this little contest of wills. I managed to push her back briefly, but eventually she managed to push the door back open. Mostly because my sock clad feet were about to slide out from under me on the wood floor and she was wearing tennis shoes and had traction out there on the porch.

"No. I'm gonna fix this ridiculousness between you and Miss Edna right now. I know both of you are too mule stubborn to be the one to make the first move. And since neither one of you drive," she gave me a hard stare, "I made the executive decision that *you're* going to *her*. In my car. Now."

I looked past her to the fifteen-year-old Ford Taurus sitting in the drive. Then I looked her dead in the eye. "Well, I'm not going anywhere in my robe. I'm buck naked under here."

She pushed past me into the house and locked the door behind her. A little shiver went up my spine. It was rare for Dixie to get in a state like this, but when she did it was best to go along with her.

The last time she got to this point was when she drove to Oxford six months after my husband passed to jerk a knot in my butt about getting back to living. Come to think of it, that had been a good decision.

Maybe this time it would be too. I sure felt awful being on the outs with Miss Edna. But wild horses wouldn't drag it out of me out loud.

I edge toward the stairs and Dixie stayed right with me. Good grief. "What? Am I going to jump out a second-story window?"

"You might just take it in your head to do it. So I'm coming upstairs with you. For all I know, you've got a rope ladder stashed up there somewhere. I'm not in the mood to chase you all over creation this morning." She put her foot on the first step.

Sighing in resignation, I turned and headed upstairs. In the walk-in closet I'd made out of a small third bedroom, I ran my eye over my clothes.

Dixie huffed out a breath behind me. "Just pick something out. It isn't a party."

I sniffed. Not a party. Of *course* it wasn't a party. But I wanted to wear something that felt right. Maybe I was just stalling for time. Maybe, deep down, I was a little scared of what might happed once we got to Miss Edna's.

I finally settled on a pair of cuffed jeans and a white button-front shirt. Nice, but not dressy uppy. I dragged out a pair of well-worn Keds from under the bed as Dixie gave me a basilisk stare.

"I'm hurryin'!"

"Well, get those shoes on and let's get this show on the road."

"Is there some kind of schedule we're on?" I asked as

I sat down to pull on the Keds.

"No," she answered. "But I've got deviled eggs in the car and I don't want them gettin' warm."

"Deviled eggs! Why?"

"Because we're all gonna sit down and have a nice brunch like civilized people." She handed me my hairbrush. "And then there are going to be some apologies made."

I pulled the brush through my hair in quick strokes. She sure was acting high and mighty this morning. "In case you haven't noticed, it's the crack of dawn. Not the time for brunch."

"It's not the crack of dawn. And at the rate you're lollygagging around, it's gonna be lunchtime before we get over there." She snatched the brush out of my hand, threw it on the vanity, took my arm and steered me toward the stairs. I felt like a child that had been actin' up and was now being punished.

I yanked my arm out of her grasp. "Now, look here. I'm not going to be the one apologizing."

She motioned toward the stairs with a frown on her face. "Come on. We're burning daylight." She started down the stairs, then turned back when she realized I wasn't following. "You will apologize." She held up a finger to stop my half-formed protest. "And Miss Edna will apologize too."

Well, *this* I had to see. I moved to the stairs and followed her down. And, if I'm honest with myself, she was right. Ugh. I hate when I've done something wrong like this.

I made a pass through the kitchen, Dixie watching to make sure I didn't run out the back, and tossed some kibble into a bowl for Elliott, my Maine Coon cat, who was meowing for his breakfast, and gave him a quick kiss and a scratch behind the ears. Poor little guy. He hadn't been getting enough attention lately, what with everything that had been going on.

Out front, as I opened the door to get in her car, I saw an insulated carrier on the passenger seat. The deviled eggs. "So, what's up with these?" I asked as I lifted the carrier off the seat.

"They're a peace offering. You know, Easter is coming up in a few weeks. Besides, I like them, and we need something to do with our hands while we're sitting around getting everything straightened out."

I stifled a laugh and gave her an incredulous look. "You take the cake for craziness." I sat and placed the carrier in my lap. The coolness of it made my thighs feel chilled in the warm morning air. Dixie got behind the wheel and we were off to see the Wizard…or at least to see Miss Edna.

We pulled up in front of her house and saw she was out on the porch. Dressed to the nines like we were company or something. Back straight, feet together, hands in her lap. That gave me pause. Being dressed up like that meant she wasn't in the mood to forgive. Not quick, anyway, like I think Dixie had planned.

But then, I had chosen my outfit with more care than I would have if everything had been fine between us and I was just dropping in. I caught Dixie eyeing Miss Edna and knew she'd just realized she had her work cut out for her. I thought I just might enjoy this.

Dixie and I strolled up the front walk, me carrying the eggs like I'd made them. I was pretty sure Miss Edna, being a savvy old woman, would know I hadn't made them. Plus, they were in Dixie's trademark red gingham carrier. The one she brought to every potluck she went to.

Miss Edna had a pitcher of sweet tea on the table with tall, cut-glass tumblers full of ice, and her second-best plates sitting there next to a quiche. Which I had no doubt at all she'd made herself while Dixie was dragging me out of my house. Score one in the gracious hostess category for Miss Edna.

"Morning, Dixie," she said as we came up her front steps. Then, with a less-than-enthusiastic look at me, she added, "Lily Gayle."

I dipped my chin just a bit in her direction. "Miss Edna."

Was that music from an old Clint Eastwood movie playing in my head? One where he stood on a dusty street in some old western town with his gun strapped on, waiting to draw? Stubborn old woman. I mentally cracked my knuckles. She and I both knew Dixie was going to get her way. It remained to be seen how it worked out.

"Well, now. Isn't this nice?" asked Dixie as she took the deviled eggs out of the carrier. She'd put them on her best deviled-egg plate—something else everyone in town would recognize because it was the carnival glass one she'd inherited from her grandma.

Miss Edna shot me a look across the table, letting me know she recognized the plate —and the fact that Dixie had made the eggs. Dixie must not have been thinkin' when she put all this together. I nodded serenely. Never let them see you sweat. Right?

"How about pouring us some of that tea while you're standing up, Dixie?" Miss Edna said. "That cut-glass pitcher gets a mite heavy for me to handle when it's full like that."

I didn't see any sign of Harley Ann and didn't want to ask about her since that happened to be the whole genesis of the mess we were trying to resolve at the moment. But Dixie had no qualms about it. She dished up three plates of food and handed them around to us.

"Did Harley Ann have plans this morning?"

Miss Edna looked uncertain, but her voice was firm as she said, "I don't rightly know. Probably out somewhere with that Moore boy." Her age-spotted hands fiddled with the embroidered linen napkin lying next to her plate of quiche and deviled eggs.

I sucked in a quick breath, and both of them looked at me. I smiled and picked up my tea, taking a sip. I sure didn't want to bring up just yet that Bobby Moore's mama had come up missing.

The three of us sat quietly eating our impromptu breakfast. Forks chimed on the little china plates as we made our way through the food. I got to feeling pretty uncomfortable with the whole situation. Anybody drivin' by would think *Well, looky there. Dixie and Miss Edna and Lily Gayle are enjoying this lovely morning together.*

When the truth was that Miss Edna and I could only glance at each other and skitter our eyes away when caught. The air felt so thick you could have cut it with a knife. I knew I shouldn't have said all that out loud when Miss Edna was trying to explain to me what had happened with Ben. But, darn it, I couldn't take it back once it was out of my mouth.

I mentally girded my loins. Time to take the bull by the horns.

"Silence is golden. But it's never been my style," I said, startling the other two. "And y'all should know that by now." I gave Miss Edna a hard look. "Especially you, Miss Edna. Because you're the same."

The sheepish look on her face said it all. Bull's-eye. I put my fork neatly across my now-empty plate and leaned forward. "Let's just go on and get this out in the open. I was surprised by what you told me, Miss Edna, and I let my mouth run without my brain being engaged."

I noticed the food in my stomach was feeling a mite trembly, took a deep breath to counter that and gave myself a pep talk. *Dixie got us this far. Do the right thing. Be the bigger person. She's an old lady. And, most of all, you love her.* "And I'm sorry for that. You were already upset and didn't need me going on like that."

I stopped for a minute, knowing I was going to risk the shaky peace I'd just achieved, but I was going to say it anyway. "Now, I'm earnest as I can be about that. And I'm going to upset everyone again with what I'm about to say."

Dixie put her hand on my arm and warned, "Don't say anything else, Lily Gayle."

But I couldn't keep my mouth shut. "Why did Harley Ann bald-faced lie to Ben about being in the woods when he questioned all of us at the café the other morning?"

Dixie started up making fluttering motions with her hands and clattering the china dishes together. Lord, I hoped she didn't break Miss Edna's second-best china. We'd both be hung out to dry for sure.

Miss Edna took the plates from Dixie's unsteady hands

and put them safely back on the table. "It's all right, Dixie. Lily Gayle's got a valid question I aim to answer. We both let our temper and pride cause trouble before. It won't happen again today."

Sitting back in her chair, she said, "First off, I want to apologize too. I wasn't myself that day. I let my thinking get all mixed up and I was too proud to be the one to apologize first." She patted Dixie's hand again. As for Harley Ann, I'm very upset with her for lying to the sheriff. But I wasn't about to bring that up at the café in front of everybody."

Heaven forbid! I thought. But I had to calm my temper down. I didn't want to ruin the shaky peace we'd gotten a start on. And, anyway, hadn't I done the same thing myself at the time?

Miss Edna went on. "The truth is, she's scared to death. And Ben coming over here and confronting her about her past was just too much."

Well, that was Ben's job, wasn't it? To catch the killer in our midst. And if he ruffled a few feathers along the way, that was just part of it. I managed to keep those thoughts to myself. It was a nice change. Maybe I'd think about doing it more often in the future.

"As I was trying to tell you the other day, Lily Gayle, my niece was convicted of driving the getaway car in a murder over in Georgia. And she spent several years in prison for it."

Dixie went all bug-eyed and put her hand to her mouth. I could see her going all gooey and *that poor girl* without her even saying anything. Miss Edna patted Dixie's hand some more in appreciation of the unspoken sentiments.

"And she paid her debt to society. She was just a young girl in love with the wrong boy. Barely eighteen. She was led astray. Why, she didn't even know that boy and his friend were robbing and murdering while she sat in the car." Miss Edna shook her head sadly. "Green as they come. But she learned a hard lesson. And now Luxen's come up dead so soon after she came here. She's scared to death she's going to get put in jail just because of her past." She glared defiantly at Dixie and me. "Harley Ann had nothing at all to do with what happened to Luxen. That's what she told me and I believe her."

I had to admit it seemed like an awful long shot that the girl would get involved in a murder here in Mercy. I mean, what could Luxen have had that she'd be interested in? Even the most skeptical jury would have a hard time believing she'd murdered him just because he wouldn't let her make and sell her butters at his bakery.

But then, he *had* been acting so very out of character when I went to see him about that. I shook my head to clear my thoughts. Too many strange happenings going on lately.

"Has Ben turned up anything in the investigation?" Dixie asked.

"Nothing so far," I answered unhappily. "It's like the murderer popped out of thin air, killed Luxen and popped back wherever he came from. Luxen led a very quiet, exemplary life here in Mercy. And the information about the camp where he came from has led to nothing. All the people have moved away over the years and no one in Tate County can recall anything from back then that might help now. No feuds. No fights. Not even a jilted girl."

Which reminded me of the conversation at the It'll Grow Back salon the day after Luxen was found. "Speaking of Luxen, Mildred says you had a crush on him back when he first came to Mercy."

Miss Edna turned tomato red. I thought she was embarrassed until she lashed out. "Mildred is a liar! And you shouldn't take anything she says as the truth." She was so upset her entire body was shaking with rage, rattling the china still sitting on the table.

Dixie's eyes met mine as a strained silence fell over the porch. She seemed as stunned as I was. Gosh. That hit a nerve I had no idea even existed. I couldn't seem to keep my foot out of my mouth.

"Circling back to Bobby Moore," said Dixie, changing the subject and breaking the tension, "did I see you going into the sheriff's department with him yesterday afternoon?"

Boy, Dixie didn't miss much. But then, the building was across the town square from her shop. And the street-to-ceiling plate-glass windows across the front afforded her a clear view of anything going on in the area.

I was glad of the change of subject. I felt bad about bringing up Mildred's comment. "Yes. His mama's missing. He came to my house yesterday, wanting me to help him look for her. I made him promise we'd go to Ben at dusk if we hadn't found her. Ben was fit to be tied when he found out Rikki had been gone for probably twenty-four hours by the time we told him about it."

"Oh, the poor thing!" Dixie said.

"I haven't heard hide nor hair from either of them." I looked at my phone to see if I'd missed a text or a call. Sometimes I accidentally put it on silent when I was rushing around and jammed it in my pocket. But nothing. I sighed. Did that mean there was no news or that Ben was on the trail of something he didn't think I needed to know? I was hoping for the latter.

Dixie jumped up from her chair. "I'm going home to fix him some food to tide him over till his mama gets home." She gathered up the plates and glasses we'd used and took them into the house.

Left alone, Miss Edna and I shared a look. I went around the table and enveloped her in a big old bear hug.

Times like this, people need to stick together.

"I'm sorry we had a fallin' out, Miss Edna. I know my own stubbornness helped cause it and I should have come here before now and owned up to it. Pigheaded pride, my mama always called it."

She hugged me back. Hard. "We're both a couple of hardheaded gals, Lily Gayle. Not necessarily a bad thing, but it can make life difficult. Be that as it may, we love each other. I'm sorry too. I know you didn't mean any harm." With a sly look and a laugh, she said, "I know you didn't make those deviled eggs."

A brief moment of irritation, we'd just made up for crying out loud, and then I laughed too. "Dixie should know better than to use her own gingham carrier and her grandma's egg plate if she's trying to fool someone."

We smiled like a couple of fools. Or friends who are glad someone intervened and helped them patch up their fight.

We were basking in our mutual admiration and our made-up differences when Dixie bustled back out on the porch. She took one look at the two of us and beamed. "Y'all made up! I'm so glad." She hugged us both. "Now, Lily Gayle, I'm gonna drop you back home and then make a couple of casseroles to take over to Bobby."

"There's another quiche I made sitting in there in the oven. Get that and take it too. Might be kind of fancy, but

I've never known a young'un that wouldn't eat it."

Dixie got the quiche and hustled me off the porch to the car. She was on a mission.

CHAPTER THIRTEEN

After Dixie dropped me off at home, I worked for a while on the Civil War gown, but I just couldn't seem to get settled in. I had gotten it to the point where everything left to do involved more exacting detail work than I could concentrate on in my present frame of mind. I didn't have a genealogy research project currently, so nothing to do there. I played with Elliot for a bit, to his obvious delight. Moved on to water my indoor plants, taking special care with the violets on the window ledge in the kitchen, wandered through the house aimlessly. Nothing caught my attention.

Going outside, I hopped on my bike and headed into town. It was a nice day for a ride, and maybe the wind would blow the tangled cobwebs from my mind. As I pedaled along in the lowering sun, I mulled over everything that had happened in the last few days. For a quiet little town, we sure had a lot going on lately.

Luxen killed; no suspects and no discernable motive. Rikki missing; again no reasons in evidence. Harley Ann with a felony record. And, for all I love Miss Edna and would trust her with my life, I had to admit to a small sense of unease about the girl. Maybe it was just the timing of it coming out; and she'd been disappearing mysteriously for hours the past couple of days. Who knew what she was up to? I pushed out a deep breath in frustration.

And the Midnight Dragonfly was still scheduled to open tomorrow evening—with that strange family in charge. I wondered if Ben had turned up any information when he went to Hernando to talk to them about Rikki. If he had, he wasn't sharing it with me. Or Bobby, as far as I knew.

For the life of me, I couldn't figure out why they bought the Mitchell place and turned it into a bed-and-breakfast. And I had to wonder how well they were going to fit in around here. But maybe they didn't care about that.

They sure hadn't made any effort to get to know anyone so far. I had to admit some of the anticipation had gone out of it for me. Of course, that didn't mean I wouldn't be there. I was still itching to get a good look at all the renovations. And we hadn't had a big town party in a long time.

I swooshed around the town square, gliding and giving my legs a little bit of a rest. It was getting to be dusk and the lights were on in the sheriff's department, where I knew Reenie was pulling her night shift as dispatcher.

The Grits and Gravy was closed. They did breakfast and lunch during the week and three meals on the weekend only. The It'll Grow Back was dark too. Dixie must still be over at Bobby's. I was glad she went. She'd be able to mother him much better than me. And maybe it'd comfort him a little bit. He must be scared out of his mind for his mama by now.

I veered off down the alley behind the stores on the north side of the town square. There was nothing beyond the asphalt delivery road but trees. Even though it was almost dark, it made for a nice, peaceful ride. As I rolled along the backside of the businesses, I ticked them off in my head in order.

Sallie's Gift Shop. I liked the homemade goat's milk soaps she sold there. So wonderful on my skin. Taylor's Drug Store. Where I ordered the crime-scene booties and special latex gloves I kept in my purse—just in case I needed them. Tibby's Titles. Our secondhand bookstore. I spent a good bit of time in there looking for new to me mysteries and thrillers. Luxen's. Where I used to get my pastry fix. He made the most marvelous eclairs. I screeched to a halt just past Luxen's, my back tire skidding sideways. Straddling the bike, I took a second look to see if the dim light had fooled me.

Nope.

The back window was up a few inches.

Don't do it, I told myself. *Ben will tear you a new one if you do.* But I ignored the voice of reason, walked my bike over to the back of the store and leaned it against the wall. I stood very still, holding my breath and listening. Nothing but crickets. So if someone had broken into the bakery, they must be gone now. Unless Luxen had left the window open for some reason in the past. But somehow I didn't think that was the case here.

I reached out, grasped the door latch and squeezed. Nothing. I squeezed harder. Still nothing. I used both hands to squeeze the latch while pulling on it sharply. Still nothing. So. Not getting in that way. I eyeballed the distance from the street up to the partially open window. It was too high for me to just hop in.

I stood directly under it, reaching up. Getting up on my tippy-toes, I could get my hands on the ledge, but just barely. I couldn't get a good enough grip to pull myself up. I jumped up a couple of times, trying to get my hands far enough in the window to catch the inside of the ledge, but the only thing I got out of it was a couple of broken fingernails and scratches on the inside of both wrists.

I stepped back, thinking, as I chewed the rough edge

off a broken fingernail. There must be a way I could get in there.

You need to hop on that bike and go report this to Ben, is what you need to do, said the voice of reason inside my head. I ignored her advice.

But, wait. The *bike*! Yes! I wheeled it so it was just below the window and leaned it against the wall. With a little prayer for success, I put one foot on the bar next to the pedals, squatted a bit, then heaved upward. Using my momentum, I put my other foot on the seat and propelled my upper body to the gap at the bottom of the window and pushed up with both hands to raise the winder higher.

Oof! As I tried to squeeze inside, the top of my head connected with the wooden frame and I felt a slight trickle of blood start along my scalp. Pushing with both hands got me past the hard part and then I was pulling myself onto a counter in the back room of the bakery. Easy-peasy.

I touched my fingertips to my scalp to check the extent of the damage. In the dim light, I saw a small amount of blood on my fingertips, but nothing to fret about. Wiping my hands down my pants leg, I surveyed the dim interior.

Dough oozed over various pans in stringy masses on several counters, evidence of loaves left to rise in the past and never finished. But I didn't smell anything awful.

The temperature in the room felt comfortable so power must still be on. I flicked a light switch, and bright fluorescents blinked on overhead like some big searchlight. Startled, I flicked the switch off, hoping no one had noticed the sudden flash of light from out on the street and picked up the phone to call the sheriff's department.

Having blinded myself with that bad decision, I felt my way along the counters, until I reached the opening onto the set of stairs that led up to the living quarters. Groping my way along the narrow passageway, I managed to arrive at the top without mishap.

Fingers crossed, I took a chance and flipped a light switch at the top of the stairs. I was in luck. It was a foyer area with closed doors, so none of the light would leak out to be seen from the street. But my dilemma was to get into the rooms without revealing myself.

I sighed. The only way to pull this off was to cut off the light in the foyer, then open the door and check to see if the blinds were closed. But once I did that, and got into the living area, I realized that even if the blinds were closed, I still couldn't turn on any lights. The blinds wouldn't cover the windows edge to edge.

I could go on and report this to Ben, or open a door to see what light might be available up here. I chose to open the door directly in front of me. A living area with a bulky couch, a man size chair and a wall mounted big screen TV revealed itself in dim lighting bleeding in along the edges of the window blinds. Courtesy of streetlights on the square just beyond the window.

It didn't look like anybody had been in here searching. At least the place wasn't all torn up with stuff dumped everywhere. It was actually as neat as a pin. I rifled through a couple of drawers in tables next to the chair and couch and a cabinet against below the TV that held movies. Nothing interesting turned up, except that Luxen favored old black and white movies featuring Gary Cooper and Jimmy Stewart. Good guy fighting back movies.

Moving into the single bedroom in the apartment, I noticed Luxen's neatness extended even here. The bed was made with a simple quilt, plain white curtains hung at the single window and no shoes or clothing littered the room. I made a thorough search of the closet, checking inside pockets and shoes. The only thing I discovered in there was Luxen favored plain clothes and shoes. No secrets hiding there.

Moving out into the room, I eased out drawers in the dresser along one wall, rifled quickly through the contents of each and found nothing. I got to the last drawer in a tall chest-of-drawers and was just thinking I should come back tomorrow when I found a photo album. This could be interesting. I took it into the bathroom with me, where I could turn on the overhead light without risk of being seen.

I squinted briefly in the harsh glare of the bathroom lighting. As soon as I got a closer look at the item in my hands, I realized the cover was discolored and brittle and I was disappointed. The album was old. With a mental shrug, I flicked through the pages anyway. There was Luxen as a young man. *My*. He *was* quite the looker back in the day. Broad shoulders and narrow hips. A wry smile on a face that could have been carved by Michelangelo.

I paused at a group shot further back in the album. Luxen was standing at the back of a group of young people. There was something about the girl standing next to him that drew my attention, but I couldn't figure out why.

I slipped the picture out from behind the protective plastic. It was the only thing I saw that seemed important. I cut off the bathroom light, slipped out the door of the living quarters and made my way downstairs and back outside. I had to leave the back door unlocked 'cause there was no way I was climbing out the window. I'd end up on my head with a concussion if I tried that trick.

I hopped on my bike and headed on over to the sheriff's department to turn myself in to Ben.

CHAPTER FOURTEEN

"For the love of God, Lily Gayle." Ben remonstrated. "How many times do I have to tell you to stop breaking and entering? You can't just go in places looking for clues."

"The window was partway up. I was worried that someone had gone in and trashed the place," I said in my own defense. "And it isn't a crime scene, so I wasn't interfering with an investigation. As a matter of fact, I found something that might be relevant to the case."

I was sitting in the visitor chair in his office, feeling like I was on trial. I'd known he'd be mad, so I just had to listen to him until he got it out of his system. But that didn't mean I wasn't going to defend myself. I crossed my legs, swinging one foot, as I waited for his next criticism.

My casual demeanor seemed to add fuel to his temper,

so it wasn't long in coming. "It's still illegal. Even if the window was unlocked. You should have come to me and I would have gone in and looked around."

"It was a citizen police act."

"We don't have a citizen police group in Mercy."

"Well, we should." I had the bit between my teeth now. "Think of all the help it could be to you!"

He rolled his eyes. "That would suit you just fine, wouldn't it? I'm more concerned about you taking the law into your own hands more than you already do than I am about missing a clue on a case. A citizen's police group wouldn't deputize you as an enforcement officer anyway. We have a tip line that works just fine."

I knew that. Really. I did. I fiddled with the picture in my hand. Ben's gaze focused on it.

"Did you take something from Luxen's apartment?" he asked in a hard voice.

I scrunched down in the chair just a little bit. I'd been so enthusiastic about my find, I'd forgotten Ben wouldn't be happy about how I acquired this interesting piece of information. I handed it across the desk.

His eyes roved over the photo and I saw the instant he recognized Luxen. Then he flipped it over, paused and said, "Did you see this on the back?"

I hadn't seen much of anything, truth to tell, because of the dim lighting while I was investigating—not breaking in—the apartment. I reached across to take the picture. Looking at the back, I realized why I hadn't noticed the writing before. It was in pencil. And faded. But still legible. *Senatobia, Mississippi, 1949. Latvian community.* Followed by a list of names. I didn't recognize a single one of them, except for Luxen.

"Does this girl next to Luxen remind you of someone? That's the reason I borrowed the picture."

He snorted, I assumed to show his opinion about me saying I'd borrowed the picture. I'd rather him do that than launch into a lecture about the definition of borrowing. I knew he wasn't done harping about me taking it on myself to investigate the open window. Nonetheless, he took the picture back from me and squinted at the image, then reached into his desk drawer and pulled out a pair of cheaters.

I smothered a chuckle at the image of him sitting there in his sheriff's uniform with the black-framed cheaters perched on his nose. Squinting despite the glasses, he angled his head, moved the picture farther away, then closer in.

"You're right. There's something familiar about her." Flipping the picture over, he scanned the names. "Maritja Riekstins." He rubbed his hand across his chin and I heard the rasp of five o'clock shadow. "Doesn't ring a bell."

He handed the picture back to me and I focused on the

girl again. Something about the shape of the eyes and the blond hair. Balancing the picture on my knees, I used my hands to block out everything except the upper part of the girl's face. And then it hit me. "Rikki Moore."

"What?"

"This girl looks like Rikki Moore!" I waved the picture around. "Or I should say, Rikki Moore looks like this girl because this picture is so old." I stood and paced around the office. "Rikki must be a shortened version of Riekstins. So they could sort of keep the family name going. She doesn't have a brother, so no boy to carry on the name."

I was so hot on the trail, my hair was practically smoking.

I rushed back to my chair, gripping the back so tight my knuckles turned pure white. "Ben! Rikki disappearing must be tied in to Luxen's murder."

"Now, Lily Gayle, don't go jumping to conclusions. I admit you've made up a plausible theory about the girl in the picture. But she'd have to be Rikki's mother. And I've never known Rikki to spend any more time around Luxen than anybody else in town. So there goes your conspiracy theory."

"I don't agree. There's got to be something there that we just haven't figured out yet."

Ben flipped the picture around, looking at the back again. He squinted some more. "Did you see this word at the end of the list of names? It's written in different handwriting. And not quite as faded. Like it was added later. Vah. True. Schkin?"

Electrified, I ripped the picture from his hands to see for myself. *Vatrushki.* The word that was in the ad for a dessert chef at the Midnight Dragonfly.

"Oh. My. Goodness! This means Rikki is tied to Luxen's murder." At the skeptical look on Ben's face, I said, "She could be a plant. Or wait… Her mother was a plant. Sent here with the other Latvians to keep an eye on Luxen and kill him. That's it! Rikki completed the assignment and now she's gone undercover until whoever is in charge comes to get her."

Ben was laughing so hard he had tears in his eyes. I gave him my best evil eye. "This isn't funny. People's lives are at stake here."

He got himself under control after a brief minute. "You watch way too much TV, Lily Gayle. Isn't that similar to the plot of that show, *The Americans*, but they're really Russian spies?"

I hesitated, thinking. I didn't watch that show, but he could be right about the premise. At least from what I'd seen on the commercials. Which was probably all he'd seen of it too.

And then I remembered the conversation with Bobby about his mama. "Ben. Remember Bobby Moore said his mama told him the people who own the Mitchell place now are Russian? How would she know that it she doesn't know them somehow?"

"She probably ran into them somewhere in town." Ben replied. "When I went down to Hernando to talk to them after she disappeared they all said they had no idea who she is."

"Well, of course they'd say that, Ben!"

"Besides," Ben said, "I don't see her running off and leaving Bobby to deal with the consequences of something illegal. Assuming anything about the conversation is true. Which it isn't."

That took the wind out of my sails. I agreed she'd never leave her son. Disgruntled that my scathingly brilliant solution had been shot down, I sat.

"Luxen had to know that Rikki was the daughter of his old friend." I circled back on the conversation.

"Why do you think that?"

I turned that over in my mind. "Don't you think he would have recognized Rikki's mom? I remember her from when we were kids, and Rikki looks a lot like her. I sat back, letting all that filter through my brain, coming up with a big fat nothing. "You really don't think it's odd that she ended up here? Married to a local boy?"

That got me thinking. I knew Rikki was born here because we grew up together. Rikki's dad was born here too. He'd left to join the service, like so many boys of his generation from small towns all over the country. It was a good living. But where had her mama and daddy met? They must have met at some military base, and when Mr. Moore left the service after twenty years, moved back here to his hometown. They'd both been in their late thirties when Rikki was born. I remembered us kids talking about it over the years because her parents were so much older than ours.

"Are we back to the Russian spy theory?" Ben asked, eyebrows raised. "Rikki's mom deliberately married Rikki's dad when she discovered the poor lonely soldier was from the town where Luxen was living? Then she came back here with him *twenty years later*, had a daughter she raised to seek retribution for some imagined crime and now Rikki has carried out her mission and gone into hiding?"

I flushed. It sounded so ridiculous when Ben said it out loud.

"I've interviewed the whole Smythe family about Luxen. Of course, they didn't have much to tell me because they hadn't been living in town during the renovations."

"Oh!" I interrupted. "That word on the back of the picture. *Vatrushki*. It was in the ad they ran in the local paper for a dessert chef."

"So now the Smythes are behind Luxen's murder?

Because of that word?"

I needed to figure out what that word is. I did a Google search on my phone and discover it was a Russian dessert.

"Well?" Ben inquired.

"It's a Russian dessert, sometimes made with cherries," I said.

"Wow. A Russian dessert. And the two oldest Smythes are Russian. I ran a background check on them just because they own the Inn. They came here from Russia after World War II and have lived all over the country. Most recently in Boston. Just like they told me. Care to make some kind of conspiracy out of that?"

My temper was starting to boil. I was tired of him talking to me like I was a fool. I was trying to help and he knew it. I stood. "I'm sick of your attitude, Benjie Carter. I'm going on home now. But I want you to think about this. Why was that word on the back of the picture and also in the ad for the dessert chef? And why was the punchbowl cake on the counter at the Midnight Dragonfly made with cherries instead of strawberries?"

He opened his mouth to reply, but I put up my hand. "Don't. Don't say one word. You just think about it."

Put that in your pipe and smoke it. Head high, I strode out of the office.

CHAPTER FIFTEEN

I was still in a state when I woke up the next morning after tossin' and turnin' all night. I rattled around in the kitchen looking for something to fix for breakfast, but nothing grabbed me, so I popped the top on a Co-Cola. I didn't drink coffee, so this was my source for caffeine. Like I needed something to get me cranked up even more than I already was.

I decided to burn off some of my bad temper working on the Civil War dress. My client would be thrilled if I got it out to her early. And maybe I'd calm down some by the time I got the final details done. Forcing myself to concentrate on the task at hand should take my mind off the mess swirling around Mercy. At least for a little while.

And maybe the break would give my poor ol' brain the change to digest everything. Who knows? If I let all the information churn around in my subconscious for a while I might end up seeing something that'd been right in front of my nose this whole time.

I was snipping off the last of the dangling threads a few hours later, admiring how well the dress had turned out, when Dixie called to ask how I was doing. "Don't get me started," I told her. She'd known me long enough to know I was in a tizzy about something. And, due to recent events, it was more than likely Ben had caused it. Wisely, she changed the subject.

"I called over to the Moors' this morning. Still no word on Rikki." She sighed. "Poor Bobby. I don't know how he's going to handle it if something bad has happened to his mama. It just beats all that she's disappeared like this with no clue."

We were silent for a moment and then Dixie went on, "And I talked to Miss Edna too. She says Harley Ann took off early this morning again and she doesn't know where the girl has gotten off to. Didn't say a word about where she's been going or what she's been up to. I can tell you Miss Edna is fit to be tied about it. Says there's been enough people wondering about her since it got out her prison sentence that it makes what ever she's doing look bad in the eyes of everybody in town."

Well. There was the kicker. I truly didn't think Miss Edna was worried that Harley Ann was up to something illegal as much as it got her goat that people in town were talking about her. What in the world was that girl up to? I wondered if it was related to Rikki going missing.

Maybe she was doing some looking around on Bobby's behalf so he could be at the house if his mama did come home on her own. Or something to do with Luxen's murder. I heard Ben in my head, clear as a bell: *Stop making everything out to be devious. Shut up, Ben.* I told that voice.

I got pulled out of my internal argument when I heard the sound of ice falling into a glass in the background. Dixie must be fixin' herself a glass of sweet tea. I noted the time on my mantel clock across the room. Three o'clock on a Saturday afternoon.

"Sounds like you're at home," I remarked. "No appointments this afternoon?"

I heard another sound in the background that I knew from experience was the footrest on Jack's big man recliner popping out. Dixie sighed. "I took off a little early today so I could come home and put my feet up for a bit before the party tonight. I'm not used to late nights anymore."

"Mercy, Dixie. You sound like some old granny. We're the same age and I'm not putting my feet up."

"From the sound of your voice, seems like you might ought to." Ice rattled as she took a sip from her glass.

"Do you a world of good to get your blood pressure under control before the party."

"You know what they say, no rest for the weary."

"I believe the correct quote is no rest for the wicked," Dixie said. "But I'm gonna let you slide on it." After a slight pause, she added, "So, what are you wearing? The invitation says cocktail attire. What does that even mean?"

"Short party dress." I sighed. "But since I haven't had a need for a cocktail dress in years, I don't happen to have one in my closet. So a nice pair of black slacks and my red silk blouse with some jewelry will have to do."

Dixie moaned. "I was afraid of that. Jack has a suit he's had for years, that still looks good on him. His weddings and funerals suit, like all the menfolk keep in their closets. But I don't have anything that has even a tiny hint of cocktail to it. I should have taken the time to run up to Memphis and get a fancy dress. Guess I'll just wear my newest summer dress with some ballerina flats."

"You'll look beautiful." I tell her. "We're not fancy people here in Mercy, so why spend hard earned money on a dress you'll probably never wear again. If the people up the hill are fancy, well that's really nothing new. The Mitchells were pretty fancy, too. I'll bring you my blue rhinestone necklace that belonged to Granny Archer to jazz up the dress a bit."

"Thank you, Lily Gayle. I really appreciate it. Can't

make a silk purse out of a sow's ear though."

"Bull feathers! You're no sow's ear Dixie Newsom. And don't you ever forget it. Besides, I don't know why we even give a hoot what they think about how we're dressed. They've been stand-offish since day one." I chuckled. "I'm really just interested in seeing how the place looks and how the other half lives. After that, I'll be satisfied. And I figure you will, too. Let's just go and eat all their food and drink all their wine while we make up stories about their lives. Like we did when we were teenagers on that school trip to Six Flags."

Dixie's sounded like she was tickled pink as she laughed into the phone. "Gracious! I'd forgot all about that trip. It was a good one for sure though. I'd best skedaddle for now. Jack and I will pick you up about six thirty. We'll be getting Miss Edna first, then swinging by your house."

I laid my phone on the side table and headed upstairs. I wasn't planning to put my feet up or take a nap, but a nice, long soak in a hot tub with a handful of honeysuckle bath salts thrown in sounded really good about now. Now that I paid attention, working on the dress had given me tight shoulders and an aching lower back. Not as young as I used to be.

Upstairs, in the master bath, I dumped a generous handful of the bath salts under the running water and inhaled as the honeysuckle scent release into the room.

Mmmmm. Almost as good as the real thing. I got them at Sallie's in town. She made them herself from an old recipe she said was handed down from her great great grandmother. I wasn't sure if that was true or a marketing gimmick she'd come up with. Either way, I'd never smelled a honeysuckle scent quite like this one.

I lit a few candles just for the heck of it. Might as well treat myself to a little spa like atmosphere. Might bring down the blood pressure Dixie had been going on about earlier. Once the tub filled almost to the brim, I cut off the water, picked up my air pillow, slid into the tub and placed it behind my head. Adjusted it to the most comfortable position and relaxed. Definitely a good decision on my part.

CHAPTER SIXTEEN

I opened my eyes an unknown time later, saw the ray of sunlight through the window had moved all the way across the room and scrambled up from the now-tepid bath water. My feet slid just a bit on the thin film left on the bottom of the tub from the bath salts.

I flailed a hand out and got a death grip on the high back of the old-fashioned soak-style tub to keep from winning the biggest splash contest in a field of one. Once I'd stabilized, I carefully lifted one foot out of the tub and placed it firmly on the thick tub side throw rug.

A close look at my hands revealed pruny fingers. Ugh. Good thing I was too nearsighted to see my feet 'cause they were probably looking pretty scary right now. I slipped on my chenille bathrobe that matched the colors in my bedroom and bath. 'Cause I'm just goofy like that.

I don't like walking around in those two rooms in a color that clashes. No problem with that in the rest of the house, though. Probably a good thing.

Just as I'd got my hair pinned up in a clip preparatory to getting started putting my face on, the doorbell rang. Well, crap on a cracker. Who can that be? It was too early for Dixie and Jack. I ignored it and started smoothing on some moisturizer. The doorbell rang again, so I gave up, cinched the belt on my robe tight and headed downstairs.

Here I went again, peering through the frosted glass panel by the door, trying to make out who was on the porch. I was seriously considering a peephole. So, some guy in brown. Looked like a uniform. I scanned out to the driveway and saw a big brown van-type vehicle. UPS? I wasn't expecting a package. After putting the chain on the door, I eased it open. Yep. UPS all right.

"Sorry to disturb you, ma'am," said a youngish dark-haired man. He averted his eyes and I thought to myself, *Yikes, old lady in a bathrobe alert.* Bahahaha! OK, I have a weird sense of humor.

"This here package was supposed to be delivered to you yesterday," he was saying, "but it slipped down behind some machinery at the sorting facility. We found it today and I'm required to get your signature."

He held out one of those electronic pads with the plastic pencil thingamajig. No way I was opening the door. Luckily, the pad was small enough that I could pull it into the house, sign and hand it back. He handed me a brown cylindrical tube, gave me a snappy salute and ran out to his truck.

I checked out the mailing label and the return address had no name and a PO box number in Hernando, MS. My red-flag antenna went up right off. Gingerly, I shook the tube. No sound. I guessed I could assume there was no bomb inside because it had been in the UPS system for a couple of days and nothing had happened.

As I started tearing off the packing tape at one end, it occurred to me there could be a bomb that only triggered when the tube was opened.

Deciding I was being silly—and my curiosity wouldn't let me wait till Ben got here—I carefully peeled the tape off the end. Nothing happened and, taking that as encouragement, I popped the plastic cap off the tube. Still no big boom. I tilted the tube, and a roll of canvas fell into my hand. It was that orangey-brown color that canvas turned when it was old. I squinted into the tube but didn't see anything else that might explain why I was receiving this package. So I unrolled the canvas.

All the blood drained from my head.

It was a kitchen scene. So very lovely in it's simplicity. Brightly colored curtains fluttered at an open window above a brown wooden table. And on the wooden table was a dish of pastries. With cherry filling oozing out onto the plate. I had a very bad feeling that the pastries were Vatrushki. There was a sheet of stationery with *Luxen's* emblazoned at the top, just above my name.

Lily Gayle,

If you are reading this, then I am dead. Or, if not, we will share a laugh together at an old man's foolish fears. This painting was entrusted to me by the artist, who was also my uncle, for safekeeping during the war. I brought it to the United States with me and have kept it hidden all these years. The artist is Kristaps Mazais, a Latvian whose work is now worth a large sum of money, and there are those who want to take it from me for their profit. I am entrusting it to your care because I believe you will do the right thing if the time comes.

Luxen

I could have screamed in frustration. Who was the villain in this murder? The Smythes? Or Rikki Moore? And was Harley Ann involved somehow? Why hadn't Luxen told me who he thought was after the painting? If he wasn't already dead I'd want to strangle him myself for being so cloak and dagger about the whole thing.

The kitchen clock chimed six, so I rushed back upstairs to get ready for the party. I quickly applied more make up than I usually wear and twisted my hair up into a messy bun with strands curling softly around my face and against my neck. Slipping into the simple black dress slacks I'd laid out earlier, I noted in relief I could still button them. I'd have been up the creek otherwise.

The bright red silk blouse was one I hadn't worn in years, but it looked great with the slacks. The deep V of the neck showing just a hint of cleavage looked sexy but not slutty. Reaching into my jewelry box I pulled out the extra long string of pearls that had belonged to my mama.

I checked my look in the mirror as I slid the pearls over my head. Not bad. If I did say so myself. I was putting my feet into the low heels I planned to wear when I heard a car honk outside.

Dixie and Jack, here to pick me up.

I grabbed Granny Archer's necklace from my jewelry box and took the stairs far too fast for the shoes I had on. Arriving at the bottom in one piece, I yanked up the seat cushion in my big club chair and carefully flattened the canvas between the cushion and bottom of the chair with the note on top. I pushed the cushion back in position and was looking to make sure everything was completely hidden when the car horn sounded again. I patted the cushion concealing the painting and note in satisfaction. I wasn't going to show it to anybody until I'd had time to think.

I picked up my small purse from the side table by the

door, dropped the necklace inside, stepped out on the porch and lock the door. Using all the motions to quiet my mind before I joined my friends. Finally I slid into the backseat next to Miss Edna and Jack pulled out of my driveway, headed out to the Midnight Dragonfly Inn grand opening.

CHAPTER SEVENTEEN

"Thanks for picking me up, y'all."

"It's no trouble." Jack answered. "Too bad Ben's working tonight."

"He said he wanted to let Todd and Mark go to the party. He doesn't care anything about it himself." I adjusted my seat belt and turned to Miss Edna. "Is Harley Ann not going to the grand opening?"

Miss Edna pursed her lips. "I haven't seen her since early this morning. She knows the party is tonight and she's a grown woman. She can find a ride if she decides to come later."

Brr. Chilly.

I caught Dixie's gaze in the rearview mirror. Her eyebrows went up. I gave a tiny headshake. I hadn't seen her either. Not wanting to talk about the painting and not wanting to stir Miss Edna up any further, I stared into the fading light of the day. It would be completely dark by the time we arrived at the party. Night still came early this time of year.

I pulled Granny Archer's necklace out of my purse and handed it to Dixie. "Here you go. Your jewels for the evening."

Even in the fading light, the blue rhinestones glittered in her hands.

Miss Edna surprised me by saying, "I remember your granny wearing that necklace, Lily Gayle. It was one of her favorites."

Dixie smiled her thanks and lower the visor so she could see the necklace as she hooked the old-fashioned clasp behind her neck. "It's lovely, Lily Gayle. Thank your for loaning it to me tonight. I'll take perfect care of it."

I was surprised when Jack slowed to a stop before we got to the turnoff for the Inn. Taking a gander out the windshield, I saw a line of car lights snaking out of sight up the drive. It was too dark to see the tags, but I swore most of them didn't look like the minimalist white-and-blue Mississippi ones.

I gave myself a mental smack. Of course, the Smythes had invited people from all kinds of places to this big event. After all, this was a business, and they sure wouldn't be a success if they depended on townsfolk from Mercy. I wondered briefly if they'd imported someone to take Luxen's place as the dessert chef.

"My goodness!" Dixie exclaimed. "I didn't expect to see all these out-of-towners."

I laughed. "I was just thinking the same thing."

Miss Edna shifted in her seat, craning her neck as she took in the sight. "I'm wishing I'd stayed home. I'm not wanting to rub elbows with a bunch of fancy people who think I'm a rube."

And there you had it. Every one of us had thought the grand opening would be locals only.

Jack chuckled. "Now, Miss Edna. We're none of us rubes."

"I know that," snapped Miss Edna. "But those people in the fancy cars are going to think so."

"Since when do you care what other people think?" Jack asked.

"Good point." Miss Edna poked him on the shoulder. "Drive on, Jeeves."

We all laughed, easing the tension in the car. At last we were parking the car in the new area to the side that Dixie and I had seen when we were up here the other day. I switched off the memories of what else we'd seen that day.

Candles in bags of sand lined the walkways and made

it appear that lightning bugs were swarming all along the edges. Very nice effect. We ambled up to the reception line, shook hands with the Smythes and moved on into the house so the folks behind us could come on in too.

The renovations knocked my socks off. Light-colored walls contrasting with the dark wood floor and soaring ceiling made for the kind of elegance we'd never seen in Mercy in the past. Sconce lighting that looked art deco had been installed all along the big hallway and the chairs and tables I'd glimpsed a few days earlier looked even better when I wasn't squinting through the blinds. Rich amethyst and tender green flowers adorned a gray background on chairs that looked like you could sit there all day. I'd give them a try later. After I'd scoped out everything to be seen.

A gorgeous grand staircase swept up to the second floor where shadows ruled the landing. Reckon we're not supposed to go up there and they didn't want to spoil the looks with blocking off the upper hallway. And the gowns and jewels on the out-of-town women made me feel like the rube Miss Edna had worried about them calling us. With a toss of my head, I put that out of my mind. They were here to visit. This was *my* home.

Miss Edna took it all in with a series of sniffs. I assumed to show her disdain for all the extravagance. Dixie said not a word, but her eyes had lit up like a child on Christmas morning and I wondered if Jack would be buying some new stuff for the house in the near future. I snuck a look at his face to see if he happened to be registering all this, but he looked the same as always. His perpetual aw-shucks smile firmly in place. Guess he hadn't notice the look in Dixie's eyes.

The three of us soon lost Jack in the crowd. No doubt to his relief. I was sure we'd find him later, off in a corner with some of the local men discussing—not gossiping about—the new Inn and its owners.

We meandered our way around the party, sampling the marvelous delicacies. I loved shrimp and grits and, somehow, they'd found someone who could create an astonishing miniature version. One perfectly cooked miniature shrimp atop scrumptious cheese grits with just a touch of gravy in a puff pastry shell. Each one a single bite of heaven. I could have eaten a whole tray and every time a waiter circulated by me with a tray of them, I snagged half a dozen without a lick of embarrassment.

Dixie just shook her head, knowing it wouldn't do a bit of good to say anything to me about it. Miss Edna kept poking me with her cane, but I just ignored her. She finally decided she'd had enough and wandered off to find Jack. I was dying to go upstairs to peek into some of the guest rooms, but a quick glance showed me the second story lights were still off and no one on the landing.

I leaned close to Dixie and whispered, "I'm dying to see upstairs. Let's find a way to get up there without anyone seeing us."

"Absolutely not," she hissed back. "We are *not* getting into trouble tonight. Jack will have a fit if we get caught."

"OK. Fine. I'm going by myself." I rambled down the hallway, looking for a way to get upstairs without using the main staircase in front of everybody. This house had been built in a time when the family had servants. Ergo, there was a back staircase around here somewhere.

"Come back here," Dixie stage whispered behind me. "I mean it."

I turned my head only to see one of the out-of-town men in a crisp tuxedo paying close attention to the two of us. Dixie gave a nervous laugh and waggled her fingers at him. He continued on and Dixie scooched to where I was standing against the wall.

"Come on, Lily Gayle. Let's just enjoy the party. There's no need to go snooping around."

I pulled her around the corner into a quieter side hallway.

"Oh, come on. Don't be a spoilsport."

She had that stubborn look on her face that drives me nuts. The one that means it's going to be really hard to bring her around to my way of thinking. I leaned against the wall for a minute to gather my arsenal. A sharp click sounded and the panel under my shoulder moved inward. I grabbed the opening to keep from falling inside. Hallelujah! A servant staircase. While Dixie was still off-balance from surprise I grabbed her wrist, jerked her into the opening with me and pushed the door shut.

CHAPTER EIGHTEEN

I pressed my ear against the door, but didn't hear any movement or shouting outside, so we must have managed to get in here without being seen. I gave myself a mental high five.

"Get that door back open right now, Lily Gayle." Dixie hissed. "You know I'm claustrophobic as hell. You know this. I'm going to suffocate in here."

I rubbed my hand over her back, like you would a child who's scared. "It's OK. This isn't a closet. Move your foot. You'll feel the stairs right next to us."

Shivering under my soothing hand, she said, "It's dark as the Devil's heart in here."

I reached out, running my free hand over the door we'd come through. There was no handle on this side. So, maybe not servant stairs. Maybe more like a secret passageway.

Cool. But also a problem. I ran my fingers all around the door trying to find a switch or recessed handle or raised section with no luck. Since I couldn't find a trigger on this side to open it, our only choice was to go up.

"I'm sorry, sweetie," I told her. "We're going to have to go up to find our way out. There isn't a latch in here. At least not one I can find."

She turned toward the door and started banging her hands against it, calling for help. I tried to stop her, but she shook me off. Pushed me so hard I landed on my butt on the stairs. Deciding it was best for the moment to stay put, I waited.

After what seemed like an eternity but probably was only a couple of minutes, she stopped. Both of us were silent, listening. Not a sound from outside. Either no one had heard all that racket or the door was soundproof.

An interesting idea that gave me all kinds of thoughts I didn't have time to examine right that minute.

Next Dixie commenced to screaming her lungs out. In the narrow space I thought my ear drums would pop from the sheer volume. Who knew she could scream like a banshee? Finally she stopped and blessed silence came back. We listened carefully at the door once more, but there wasn't a whisper of sound outside.

"Come on," I said to her at last, standing up from my seat. "Let's follow the steps up. We'll get out once we get to the top."

"I swear, Lily Gayle Lambert, when we get out of here I'm going to beat you to death."

On that positive note, we climbed. In total darkness, both hands against the walls to each side. Each step tentative at first, then when I felt confident, pressing upward again. I didn't mention it out loud, but I was having some anxiety about getting out of here at the top. What if I couldn't find the trigger up there either? I'd hate to try and make our way back down in this pitch blackness.

Going down a set of stairs is always more dangerous than going up. Especially when you can't see your hand in front of your face and your best friend is breathing hot air on your neck.

I kept these thoughts to myself. No sense in getting Dixie even more upset.

We found the door at the top simply because we ran into it headfirst. On a landing barely big enough for both of us to stand on, we rested for a minute in silence, both of us dragging musty air into our lungs. My thighs burned like fire from the steep climb of these interior stairs.

"Get to finding the way out of here, Lily Gayle." Commanded Dixie. "I'm serious as a heart attack. I'm so mad I could push you right down these old stairs and not regret it."

I put my hands out and felt around the wood in front

of me. Praying the whole time I'd trigger the door open by sheer good luck. Just like I did downstairs. Although I didn't think Dixie considered any of this to have been good luck. Praying under my breath, I kept running my fingers along what felt like the edges of a door.

The indention was so tiny I thought I'd dreamed it at first. Moving my fingers back to that spot I mashed in. No results. I felt a layer of sweat break out along my hairline. Next, I pushed down and heard a quiet click, and the panel swung out an inch. *ThankyousweetbabyJesus.*

Dixie wasn't waiting for an invitation. She pushed me up against the wall and face-planted out into a dim room. Peeling myself off the wall, I stepped into the room, paused to yank the back of Dixie's dress down over her panties, and looked around. Dixie rolled to her feet and stood next to me.

Unable to believe my eyes, I blinked twice, looked around the room, then focused back on the original spot.

Across the room, Rikki Moore was hog-tied to a chair with Harley Ann standing over her holding a butcher knife big enough to slaughter a calf.

Rikki focused eyes as big as silver dollars on me and hollered behind the gag in her mouth. Harley Ann turned, saw Dixie and me and started toward us. We stepped back involuntarily. I mean, when someone is coming at you with a butcher knife it's just natural. Then Harley Ann, burst into tears.

"Thank God y'all are here!" She sobbed. "I don't know how I'm gonna get her out of this house."

Waving the knife around, Harley Ann launched into a fit of babbling so bad I couldn't make out a word she was trying to say.

"For cryin' out loud, give me that knife before you hurt somebody." I took it gingerly from her hand.

"Now, the big party is going on down stairs, so I think we're safe for a bit. Take a deep breath and start at the beginning."

Harley Ann blinked, swallowed and said. "I wanted to help Bobby find his mama." She turned teary eyes to Rikki, then back to me. "I knew she didn't have a real high opinion of me after my past got out all over town. So, I thought if I could be the one to find her, then I'd stand taller in her opinion."

She sniffled, wiped her face with the heels of her hands and continued. "So, I thought about everything that happened. And I asked Bobby a bunch of questions about his mama. When he told me she'd said these folks up here are Russian, and Miss Edna had told me what you found out about the Latvian group and how Luxen was one of them, I decided to come up here and do some investigating."

I could just picture Ben's reaction to all this once we

got out of here. He'd be fit to be tied when he found out Harley Ann was going to be just as curious as me about crimes. And, from the way she'd put together the information, pretty good a solving them. She'd make a great addition to our group.

"Couldn't you find anything smaller than this?" I asked sarcastically, referring to the knife as I marched over to Rikki and cutting her loose from the chair.

She reached up, untied her gag and proceeded to cough up a bunch of blood and mucus. There was a cut on the side of her mouth that must have bled into her throat while she'd been up here. I helped her back into the chair before she fell down. Dixie disappeared into a connecting bathroom, bringing back a cup of water she handed to Rikki.

"Go on." I said to Harley Ann. "How did you find Rikki in here?"

"Well," Harley Ann said. " I snuck in the back door when the caterers weren't looking because I though I might find some clues up here on the second floor. And I just grabbed the first knife I saw as I was coming through the kitchen. In case I needed to protect myself."

She looked at Rikki. "I never dreamed Miss Rikki was tied up in here. I've been hiding out up here all day, checking room by room and I'd just come into this room to look around and found her when y'all busted through the wall over there."

Rikki set the cup of water on the floor next to her. "I'm never gonna be able to forgive myself." Tears streamed down her cheeks. "If it weren't for me, Luxen wouldn't be dead."

I thought of the painting he'd sent to me. And the note. "That's not true, Rikki."

"It is," she insisted. "I told Viktor and Sergei that Luxen had the painting they were looking for. They found me first. They used their plan to buy a property to open a bed-and-breakfast to look through all the small towns around here. They knew about the Latvian camp after the war, and somehow, they traced me here. They thought I had the painting."

She wiped her face with shaking hands. "I was so scared. The only thing I could think was that they'd go after Bobby if I didn't cooperate. So I told them about Luxen." She hung her head. "I tried to steer them somewhere else to throw them off until I could warn Luxen. But he wouldn't listen to me and leave town. And now he's dead. And then, when they couldn't find the painting at Luxen's bakery or apartment, they came to my house and kidnapped me. I told them over and over I didn't know anything, but they kept insisting I did. "

Dixie went to her, hugging her close. "It's not your fault, Rikki."

"Dixie's right," I said. And I told her about the package at my house. "Right now, we need to get you out of here."

"How are we going to do that without them seeing us?" Harley Ann asked.

I grinned. "Ladies. We aren't going to sneak out of here. We're going out the front door like we own the place."

The four of us stood at the head of the main staircase, looking down into the crowd below. Jack stood openmouthed close to the front door with Miss Edna and Bill Johnson next to him.

The two elder Smythe men moved to the bottom of the stairs as if to block our escape. The grandson and his wife tagged along behind, confused expressions on their faces.

"My mama taught me never to throw the first punch, but y'all can bet your bippies I'll be throwing the last one if needed. Come on, ladies, rush 'em."

As one, we swarmed down the staircase right at the Smythes. I heard Brenda Smythe asking what was going on just before we crashed into them, knocking the men to the floor. And none of us threw a single punch.

CHAPTER NINETEEN

I glanced at Miss Edna and Harley Ann sitting next to each other, smiling. And I was glad. Glad to be sitting here with my closest friends on a beautiful morning. Glad all the mysteries had been solved and glad the girl had justified her great-aunt's faith in her. She had a walking cast on her foot, which got broken in the fracas at the bottom of the stairs the night before. But I don't think she has any regrets about it. She'd sealed her place with Bobby Moore, if she wanted it, by saving his mama. Not a bad night's work on her part.

We had our glasses of sweet tea close at hand as we rocked and hashed over what had been happening for the past week. It seemed a lot longer that that. Funny how things can turn on a dime like that.

"Lily Gayle. Dixie. I'm sorry for that conniption fit I

had about Mildred being a liar," Miss Edna said. "I want to clear up what that was about. Luxen and I truly were in love back when we were young, but he said he could never marry me. I guess it still doesn't set right with me. Even all these years later. He wouldn't tell me why and, not being a very confident young woman, I thought it was something about me. I understand why now. I just wish he'd known he could have told me the truth all those years ago. I know, now, he thought he'd be putting me in harms way if we'd married."

Harley Ann took that moment to redirect the conversation into safer waters. "Remember how Missy told us last week at breakfast that she took the Smythes on a tour of Mercy and it seemed like that was when they decided to buy the Mitchell place? That stuck in my head for some reason. And when Miss Rikki went missing, I decided there was a connection somehow. They saw the bakery sign and knew Luxen lived here. That's why they chose Mercy." She was quiet for a minute. "If he hadn't put his name on the front of the bakery like that, they'd never have found him."

I glanced at the painting I'd brought over to show them. Something so lovely that had caused death and misery. But we were going to make it right. At least, as right as it could be made. I'd looked up the artist via the wonders of the internet and discovered the painting, a rare pre-WWII canvas by a Latvian citizen, was now worth millions.

"I talked to Rikki about the painting, and we're going to contact someone at the Latvian National Museum in Riga about returning it," I told them. "It belongs there. I think Luxen would like that."

"So what did Ben discover when he hauled that bunch into jail last night?" Dixie asked.

I blew out a breath. "It's a pretty crazy story. I guess the two oldest guys knew it was the end of the trail for them. Sergei told Ben that the his son and daughter-in-law had no idea they were being used as cover for for a covert hunt being orchestrated by his father."

"Balderdash!" said Miss Edna.

I laughed. "At first I thought the same. But after I heard the whole story, I can see where they might not have been in the loop on it. It was an obsession for the old man. One he refused to give up and his son went along with him to keep the grandson out of it. Seems that was the agreement between the two of them."

"But why were they after Luxen in the first place?" asked Harley Ann.

"According to Sergei, Kristaps Mazais," I stumbled over the unfamiliar name and at the puzzled looks of the others tapped my fingers along the edge of the painting. "The artist. Anyway, Viktor was going around stealing artwork in Latvia during World War II and Kristaps stood up to him. That drove Viktor nuts, so he beat up Kristaps and took all the painting in the studio. But later found out there was one other one that Kristaps had given to his nephew to sneak out of the country."

At the looks of disbelief on the faces of the others, I said. "I know. It seems beyond comprehension. Apparently the obsession didn't really take hold until a few years ago. Guess Viktor realized he wasn't going to live forever and wanted to get that done before he kicked off. Who knows how the minds of crazy people work."

"I thought they were already rich. Why did he need that painting?" Harley Ann puzzled.

"I don't think it was about the money. I think it was about someone who got something over on Viktor and he couldn't stand it."

"How'd they even get into the United States with that kind of background?" Miss Edna asked indignantly.

"Ben said they probably had false documentation. He said it's happened before and he figures it's the case here. He called the FBI and they'll be down here later today to take them all into custody while they sort out who knew what and when they knew it."

"I wonder what'll happen to the Inn," Dixie said. "Jack drove up there with Ben to help board it up. Seems a shame after all the renovations and how beautiful it looks now."

"I figure it'll go up for sale again. It's truly possible the grandson and his wife didn't know what the other two were doing, but there's no way they can operate the Inn after everything that's happened. They'd be run out of town on a rail if they ever came back here."

"Oh!" said Dixie. "I just realized. Luxen was trying to leave a clue that last day he was up at the Inn."

"What do you mean?" I asked.

"The cake. It was cherry instead of strawberry. And we never caught on to that."

Author's Note

There was a real Latvian camp in Tate County, Mississippi, from approximately 1949 to 1953. The individuals who lived there, sponsored by a resident of Senatobia, Mississippi, who was an officer stationed in Germany at the end of the war, came to the United States via ship to the Port of New Orleans and then traveled north to Senatobia. Once they had worked for two years, mostly raising cotton, to pay back their sponsor, the majority moved to other parts of the country in search of other Latvian communities and climates that were closer to that in their home than the torrid Southern summers in North Mississippi. There's a marker in Senatobia honoring these displaced persons and the mark they left on a small community. I have taken artistic license with the characters in this book. None of the real displaced

Latvians were involved in any thefts or criminal activity relating to stolen artwork from Latvia or Russia.

If you enjoyed this book, I'd really appreciate a review on Amazon. The number of reviews a book has is a direct impact on sales. So just leaving a review, no matter how short, it can be one word, helps make it possible for me to continue writing more books. Please click here to leave a review: http://ow.ly/u7wd30aa5GU

(Death by) Chocolate Gravy

1 cup sugar

4 tbs. flour

4 tbs. cocoa

2 cups milk

½ stick butter

2 tsp. vanilla

Mix sugar, flour and cocoa together and place in iron skillet. Slowly add milk while whisking briskly. Heat on medium high until bubbly. Turn down, stir continuously and simmer till thickened to desired consistency. Add butter and vanilla. Stir to combine and serve over hot biscuits.

Wicked Chickens Deviled Eggs

6 eggs
2 tbs. mayo
2 tsp. yellow mustard
½ to 1 tsp. dill pickle juice
Salt and pepper to taste
Paprika for tops

Place 6 eggs in a 2-quart pot with enough water to cover eggs and bring to boil.

Remove from heat 12 to 15 minutes after they start boiling. Boiling eggs too long will result in a dark ring round the yolk

Drain hot water and place boiled eggs in ice bath for about 10 minutes.

Remove each egg from ice bath and peel. Hold egg under slightly warm water from faucet to make peeling easier.

Slice peeled eggs in half lengthwise.

Scoop out yolks into mixing bowl.

Add mayo and mustard to yolks and mash well with a

fork.

Add dill pickle juice a little at a time until you reach the taste you like.

Add salt and pepper to taste.

Scoop mixture into egg halves with a teaspoon.

Sprinkle tops with paprika.

Place on deviled egg plate, cover with Saran Wrap and chill in refrigerator.

Decorate with parsley sprigs.

Punchbowl Cherry Cake

Deep clear glass bowl
1 box white cake mix
1 (6 oz.) pkg. vanilla instant pudding mix
2 large bananas
1 large can crushed pineapple (drained)
2 (10 oz.) pkgs. frozen cherries
1 large container whipped topping

Follow instructions on cake mix and bake in 9 x 13 pan. Set aside to cool. Make instant pudding and place in refrigerator to chill. Peel and slice bananas. Remove cake from pan and cut into chunks. Place layer of cake pieces in bowl followed by ⅓ of pudding, ⅓ of pineapple, ⅓ of cherries and ⅓ of banana slices. Spread a layer of whipped topping. Continue layers until all ingredients are used. Finish with whipped topping. Place in refrigerator to chill overnight. Serve cold with whole cherries on top.

**For a 4th of July theme, replace cherries and pineapple with strawberries and blueberries.

**Can also substitute chocolate instant pudding for the vanilla.

Mmm Mmm Good Chicken Fried Chicken with Pan Drippins' Gravy

4 boneless skinless chicken breasts

1 cup flour

½ tsp. salt

½ tsp. pepper

3 eggs

Vegetable oil

Place chicken breasts between pieces of plastic wrap and pound till evenly flattened. Whisk eggs in separate bowl. Mix flour, salt and pepper together in brown paper bag. Dip each piece of chicken in the egg mixture, place in paper bag and shake to coat. Remove from bad, shake off excess and place on plate. Dip in egg mixture again and place in paper bag to coat again. Shake off excess. Do this for each piece of chicken.

Put enough vegetable oil in an iron skillet so that the depth is about one inch. Heat oil. When oil is hot, place chicken in the skillet. Cook till golden brown.

Pan Drippins' Gravy

¼ cup pan drippings
¼ cup flour, seasoned with salt and pepper
1 ¼ cup milk

Drain all but about ¼ cup of the oil from the pan. Be sure to leave the crumbles from cooking the chicken, use a spatula to scrape them lose. Sprinkle ¼ cup of flour slowly over the drippings. Stir until light brown. Slowly add the 1 ¼ cup milk, whisking continuously. Bring to a boil, reduce heat and let simmer until gravy reaches desired consistency. If it gets too thick for you, whisk in milk a little at a time until desired consistency is reached.

Serve chicken with gravy spooned over the top. Top with a little black pepper if you like.

Made in the USA
Columbia, SC
24 November 2017